FLICKER WORLD

BRIAN CRAMER

FLICKER WORLD

Published by Brian J. Cramer
www.briancramerbooks.com

ISBN-13: 978-0-9961529-4-5
ISBN-10: 0-9961529-4-6

Dedicated to my brother
Richard Cramer.

His determination to forge a
new career in a profession that
he enjoys continually inspires
me to do the same.

CHAPTER 1

---▼---

It was a rainy Tuesday night and Lisa was once again working by herself in the lab after hours. As an experimental chemist, she enjoyed the distraction-free solitude of the night shift. It was a perfect time to let her mind wander like a leaf on the breeze, flitting here and there, drifting anywhere the gentle currents of thought would take it.

Tonight, on a whim, she had decided that it was going to be a random mixer night. To a social climber, this might have meant going to a party with cocktails in order to meet new people, but Lisa had a different idea in mind.

It is said that many of mankind's greatest discoveries were the result of mere accidents. Lisa therefore reasoned that her pathway to higher achievement lay in creating an opportunity for as many accidents as possible.

To that end, she began her mixer by walking into the middle of a C-shaped counter, the top surface of which had been covered with test tubes by one of her assistants earlier in the day. She pulled out a pair of dice from the pocket of her lab coat and tossed them onto the counter. She rolled a "4" and a "2".

Tilting her head slightly, she said to herself, "OK, so we are going for six today." She then closed her eyes tightly and spun herself around a few times in the center of the space surrounded by the circular counter. After steadying herself against the slight dizziness, she cautiously walked forward until she reached the edge of the counter. She then walked clockwise around the counter while selecting six test tubes at random.

With the test tubes in hand, Lisa opened her eyes and took the samples to a lab bench where, after first turning on the vent hood and donning protective gear, she began to mix random but carefully-weighed portions of each sample into a flask. She recorded the weights of each sample into a hand-held electronic tablet before each pour.

These six samples could have been anything, be it animal fat, sulfuric acid, herbal tea, or water from a puddle outside. Each test tube had a number on it instead of the specimen's name to curb any bias in Lisa's selection process. Lisa's assistant would have had an index that listed each ingredient by name and number in case Lisa had a "eureka" moment and needed to replicate the mixture.

Tonight's mixture, however, did not result in such a moment. As the mixture thickened and turned dark brown inside the flask, it released a bubble of noxious gas accompanied by a sickly "blurping" noise.

Lisa took a quick step backwards. This was clearly more of a "you-reek-uh" moment. She fanned the fumes away from her nose with her hand and took another step back.

A voice from behind her said, "That's really dangerous, you know."

Lisa yelped and spun around. Instead of the angry demon from the netherworld that she had expected, standing behind her was her coworker, Sharon, who had come back to ensure that Lisa was not doing anything to endanger herself or the lab.

It must be said, however, that when Sharon was genuinely angry even a demon from the netherworld would probably run from her. It was therefore fortunate for Lisa that Sharon appeared to be in a jovial mood.

Lisa folded her arms and frowned at her friend. "Don't scare me like that," she said with a pout.

Sharon ignored this and continued, "I thought we agreed that we weren't going to do Russian Scientist Roulette when no one else was around? What if you were knocked out by the fumes? Or... what... if..." She trailed off as she watched the flask behind Lisa as its contents started to hiss and overflow from the container. She quickly grabbed Lisa's arm and pulled her away.

Lisa turned around to see what was the matter. She saw the flask being carried away by a thick stream of smoking brown ooze. "Oh," she said with a mixture of calm and disappointment, "I see."

There is a type of firework called a black snake. It starts as a small black pellet but when it is lit on fire it forms a long snake of ash. The flask was replicating this to a larger scale in brown sludge. The two scientists ran out of the lab and sealed the door behind them.

Out in the hallway, Sharon turned to Lisa and said, "Look, I know that the company hired you for this special 'Dreamers' program, and I know that you are meant to push the envelope even more than the research and development nerds, but you are still a scientist just the same. Try not to be so damn stupid next time, would you?"

"Yes, dear," answered Lisa with a sigh.

Sharon made a face. "And don't treat me like I'm your nagging wife."

"Yes, dear."

Sharon shook her head and grabbed Lisa's arm. "Come on, let's take a break and go to the cafeteria."

Lisa stayed planted and shook her head while saying, "Oh, no. Not now. Haven't you heard? They say that the lunch room is haunted between the hours of one and six in the morning."

Sharon rolled her eyes. "I'm sure they say that just to keep you from eating all the candy bars. Anyway, who is they?"

"You know," answered Lisa while waving a hand in the air, "they... people... everyone."

"Ah, well, you can't go around listening to them. And explain to me how a skeptically-minded scientist has wound up believing in ghosts? And it isn't just ghosts, is it? I mean, last week you swore up and down that the government was training trout to assassinate the president of Uzbekistan."

"Shh," answered Lisa while nervously looking around. "Don't let them know that you know, or it might never be safe for you to go swimming again."

"Well? I'm still waiting for an answer," said Sharon, determined not to get sidetracked.

Lisa thought about this and then explained, "Science is not just about working with things that you know and understand, science is about speculating on the unknown, about probing the very edge of our knowledge and constantly testing our assumptions."

"Yes, yes," said Sharon dismissively. "You would make a very good marketing person since all you are doing now is spewing meaningless tripe. But sure, OK, science is all about finding out new things, and pushing the boundaries of this and that, but it is also about holding up that new information and comparing it to the body of knowledge that we already possess, and then being able to say, 'You know what — this new information is complete and utter crap.'"

Lisa's forehead creased in thought. After a few seconds she said, "So what you are saying is, you think that it is probably safe for me to get a chocolate bar from the cafeteria?"

Sharon smiled and gave Lisa a halfhearted laugh. "Exactly. Now, let's go." She tugged again on Lisa's now unresisting arm and led her to the cafeteria.

After helping themselves to some snacks, the two scientists resumed their earlier conversation while sitting together at a table.

Sharon asked again, "So, why do you believe in ghosts? You still haven't given me a straight answer."

Lisa took a bite of her chocolate bar and chewed thoughtfully. She swallowed and said, "Well, it all started two months ago. You remember me saying that I felt like I was being watched, right?"

"Yes," agreed Sharon. "I remember you saying that you thought Russian spies were watching you, and before that you said it was aliens."

"True," Lisa conceded. "Those were my hypotheses at the time. But in the face of new evidence, I have changed my mind."

"What new evidence?" asked Sharon, leaning forward slightly.

"I saw it. I saw the ghost."

"Get out!"

Lisa shook her head. "No, I'm serious. Things have been getting really weird at home the last two months. At first, like I said, it began with just the feeling of being watched. Sometimes I would catch my cat staring over my shoulder with her pupils so dilated that they looked like two pools of ink."

"Yes, well, cats do that sort of thing," said Sharon, dismissively.

"They do," agreed Lisa, "but that doesn't mean that there isn't a reason behind it. Cats see differently than we do. I think he was able to see the ghost before I could."

"OK, so what happened next?" asked Sharon, who was getting interested despite herself.

Lisa continued, "A few days later, I had that same sensation again — of being watched — but before I could turn around to investigate, I felt a slight pressure around my shoulders while something lightly brushed against my face."

Sharon asked wide-eyed, "What did you do?"

"I screamed. Then the pressure went away. After I had calmed down, however, I realized that I was not really scared of it. Sure, it had taken me by surprise, but it did not seem malevolent to me. In fact, it felt warm, sort of like being hugged by someone that missed me. Is that weird?"

Sharon narrowed her eyes. "Yes..." she said, "but I believe you. I've never known you to lie. You said that you actually saw this thing, right? So I'm guessing it came back."

"Correct. A few days later I was watching this reality TV show when the television suddenly changed channels to a program about meerkats."

"What did you do?" interrupted Sharon.

"I watched it. It was very interesting. They have a whole little society, those meerkats. It was sort of like watching a soap opera. There was this one little guy that..."

"Fascinating," interrupted Sharon again, "but what about the ghost?"

"It was sitting on the couch next to me," answered Lisa, simply.

"It was what?"

"Sitting next to me. I could just barely see it, but I could definitely feel the pressure of it against my body. At one point it felt like it was stroking my hair."

"What did you do?" asked Sharon again.

"I let it."

"You... let it?"

Lisa nodded. "It was nice, in a way."

"Lisa, sweetie, darling, we really have to find you a man. This isn't healthy."

"It's not like that," protested Lisa. She looked down at the table. "Besides, no one is really interested in me. No one understands me. I'm pretty sure that I'm supposed to be alone. They say that there is someone out there for everyone, but for me, I can't help thinking that my someone is missing."

Sharon walked around the table and gave Lisa a hug and a kiss on the cheek. "Well, you always have me."

Lisa smiled while rubbing her cheek dry with her shoulder and then pushed Sharon away jokingly. "Get away, you big goof."

Sharon smiled back and returned to her seat. "So, back to this ghost lover of yours. What happened next? You two went to see a movie together? He didn't take advantage of you, did he?"

"No, nothing like that," said Lisa, blushing slightly. "I felt its presence a few more times that week and then it disappeared for some time. I thought it was gone forever. It actually made me a little sad. But then, a week later, I heard someone calling my name."

"Did it say anything else?"

Lisa frowned. "It just said, 'Lisa! Lisa! It's me. Can you hear me? Oh hell.' Then it disappeared again. It had a male voice."

"It's me?" Sharon parroted. "That's not very helpful. Any idea who it was? Someone you used to know that has since died?"

Lisa shook her head. "No, no idea at all. That's the weird thing. I didn't recognize the voice at all. I don't have many male friends. Certainly none that have died. It's very puzzling."

"So what happened after that? Did you see it again... him?"

"Yes. It was at night again, just like all the other encounters. I couldn't sleep so I went out back for some fresh air. I saw some weeds in the garden, which bothered me, so I started to do some weeding. I was halfway down a row when I realized that the next weed had already been pulled, as were all the others. It was then that a voice just behind me said, 'I couldn't just stand here and not help.'"

Sharon inhaled quickly.

Lisa continued, "I turned around, and there he was — a figure of a man, blobby, white, and slightly fuzzy. It was like looking at a negative of a shadow."

"Oh my god. What did you do?"

"I was brave. I talked to him a little, but then he suddenly had to go."

Sharon laughed. "Casper the bashful ghost, eh? Did he ever come back?"

Lisa's eyes glanced over Sharon's shoulders for a moment at something on the other side of the cafeteria. She took a deep breath, lowered her voice slightly, and said, "Actually, that's where it gets interesting. I didn't want to bring this up until you heard the whole story. I didn't want you to be alarmed. But the thing is... well, the ghost... now don't be alarmed... but the ghost... he's actually here, now. And he's walking towards us as we speak." Lisa pointed at something just over Sharon's right shoulder.

Sharon stood up so fast that her chair went sailing backwards and toppled over. She spun around. There was nothing there.

Lisa laughed. "Gotcha!"

CHAPTER 2

▼

Mark was daydreaming as he sat on the toilet. He had just graduated from college a few short months ago and now it was time for him to go out into the "real world" and it was making him nervous. Today he was going to a job fair hosted by several big shots in the so-called military industrial complex. All the big boys like Lockheed Martin, General Dynamics, and Raytheon were going to be there as well as a handful of scrappy upstarts.

Mark was really hoping to dazzle someone into giving him a job today. He knew that he had the grades to back him up, but probably so did everyone else at the fair. To gain an edge, he felt he needed to be confident and charming, but all he could muster right now was nervous and apprehensive.

He stared down at the heater vent on the wall in front of him. He could just make out a tiny little spider floating on an invisible web strung in front of it. Mark said, "You can't stay there too much longer, little guy. Things are going to get very hot for you come winter." He made a mental note to move the spider before then if it happened to still be around.

Evidence notwithstanding, Mark was not fond of insects, and that went double for spiders. He tolerated this one, however, since it was very small, did not put webs anywhere that Mark walked, and caught other more menacing bugs.

One might wonder why someone like Mark, who by all accounts would literally not hurt a spider even though he did not like them, was going to a job fair hosted by warmongers? The answer, of course, was money. Mark knew that private research jobs were few and far between in America, and even if he did find one, chances were that they were probably with a venture capital firm that was not likely to be around for more than a year or two.

He was well aware of the usual fate of that sort of company, especially the ones in his area. They tended to burn out quickly once the money had run out and the founders realized that despite all of the meetings, the trans-continental flights, and the huge bonuses for meeting key goals, they had not actually, in fact, produced anything.

Mark might have been OK with a temporary job like that if he only had to worry about himself, but now that he was engaged, he had to think about long term stability.

It had become evident to him from watching the steady flow of disturbing news reports that world peace was very unlikely to be achieved in his lifetime, and that the government — and by extension the military — was likely to be the last entity to run out of funds since people in control with very big guns usually get whatever they wanted. Well, at least until there was so little left to take that the civilians finally got fed up and start showing a keen interest in pitchforks, torches, and guillotines.

At any rate, Mark was as fond of the military as he was of spiders, but like the spider, he would bear with it if it proved useful. Besides, he told himself, he would not be working directly with the military, but rather for a civilian subcontractor.

He just hoped that whomever he ended up working for was not going to have the same mindless regimentation as the military. After all, you couldn't very well have a functioning research facility if you had a culture that stamps out individuality and promotes unthinking obedience.

Mark put his doubts aside for the time being and finished in the bathroom. He said goodbye to the spider and imagined that it gave him a tiny little thumbs up.

As Mark walked into the kitchen, his mother grabbed him by the shoulders and said, "Oh, look at you! My little boy is all grown up." She straightened his tie, which had already been straight.

Mark sighed. Nothing makes you feel more manly than your mother straightening your tie, he thought.

At about that time, Mark's father stepped into the kitchen from the living room and gave him one of those big, fatherly pats on the back that are supposed to be loving and reassuring, but are really just annoying, awkward, and sometimes even painful.

Mark's best friend, Pryb, had once explained to Mark that he had actually come from a dysfunctional family because, these days, being from a family where your parents were still not only together but also actually loved one another and their children was so rare as to be something shameful that should be hidden from the rest of society. Pryb, on the other hand, had come from a healthy background with an exotic dancer for a mother who used to leave his lunch money on the table for him in folded dollar bills, and an alcoholic father who only sent him a card once a year around Christmas time, usually asking for money.

Mark reflected on that while he was being fully emasculated by his mother as she smoothed down his cowlick with some saliva and his father smacked him on the butt while Mark tried to walk out of the house with some dignity.

As he walked to his car, his parents were yelling out to him about how proud they were of him for serving the good of the country and wished him luck.

In his head, he could imagine his best friend's voice saying, "You know, good parents would be scolding you right now and telling you not to waste your talents on stuff that is meant to kill people and break things. My dad would have smacked me on the head and pushed me down the stairs by now. It's like your parents don't even care about you. It's very sad."

Mark used the hour-long drive to Sacramento as an opportunity to make himself even more nervous. By the time he had made it to the National Guard campus, he was so nervous that he was ready to give up and go back home. However, when he thought about how much he loved Lisa and about how disappointed she would be if he came back without a job, he forced himself onward.

As he walked toward the first booth, he reminded himself that his only real hope in standing out in the crowd was to be as charming and likable as possible.

Mark walked up to the woman at the Blackhawk booth and asked her if there was any cotton candy at this fair. She gave him a strange look and reluctantly handed him an application to fill out. Mark had only been pretending to have stupidly mistaken this as a normal fair as a joke, but this had evidently backfired since it had been interpreted as genuine stupidity.

Mark stared at the paper application and wondered why in the 21st century this process had not yet been automated. Surely he should just be able to hand the lady a memory stick with his resume on it and call it a day.

Damn! He thought, that reminds me that I forgot my resumes at home. He started to sweat. This is not going well at all, he thought.

The woman politely waved him aside and took the next applicant. He was pretty sure that he had flubbed that one, but he was not unduly concerned because he actually wanted to land a job at one of the smaller companies. He was cutting his teeth on the big boys now just to get a feel for things. Once he had some practice, he would try his luck with his intended targets.

At the Lockheed booth, he at least got a chuckle from the old man when he asked for cotton candy. The man said, "No, sorry young man, no cotton candy, but we do have some chocolate." He handed Mark a small chocolate bar wrapped in a golden wrapper with the Lockheed Martin logo imprinted on the front in black ink.

Mark popped the chocolate in his mouth and then sang (with a mouth full of chocolate), "I've got a golden ticket..."

"Yes, very good," said the old man, dismissively. He looked past Mark and called out, "Next, please."

While walking away, Mark gave the old man a thumbs up and said, "Thanks for the chocolate."

Well, things are going well so far, Mark told himself. He was scanning the fair for his next target when a voice suddenly called out from behind him, "Mark Scottsdale? Get out of town. Is that really you?"

Mark spun around. "Holy cow, Steve Bestiality! How the hell are you? What brings you here? You looking for a job from these soulless warmongers too?"

"Oh yes, it's you alright," said Steve while reaching for Mark's hand to shake. "Firstly, it's Bastille, you bastard, and you know it. Secondly, No, I'm not looking for a job — I'm offering one. As for soulless warmonger..." Steve bobbed his head this way and that "... eh, you probably got me there."

"Wait, what? You work for one of these guys?" asked Mark.

Steve pointed at Mark with both hands and said, "No, I don't work for any of these clowns. I'm the boss. He pointed over his left shoulder at another booth and said, "That's me over there... Accelerated Technologies, or AccelTech for short."

Mark nodded. "Good name... Good name. I see that 'C' in marketing really paid off. So, wow, how did all this come about?"

"It's funny you should ask that," replied Steve. It's all thanks to you, in fact."

"What?"

"No, it's the god's honest truth. Walk with me. Let's get some lunch and I'll tell you all about it."

"But," protested Mark, "I still have to find a job first. How about we meet up later for dinner instead?"

Steve made a face. "Job shmob. Forget these clowns. Look, you want a job, I'll give you a job. Boom. Done. Now, let's go get some lunch, alright?"

"Wait, what?" asked Mark.

"You mean, wait, what, sir."

Mark made a face. "Do I really have to call you sir?"

Steve wiggled his hand. "Eh, only around the others. You, know, for the look of the thing."

"Thanks, man. I really appreciate you giving me a job. You have no idea how much this helps me," said Mark enthusiastically. "So, how much..."

"Eh, eh, eh," interrupted Steve. "Not here. All in good time. Let's go to lunch and talk things over."

Mark nodded.

Steve led them to the parking lot where a black Escalade with black windows had been waiting for them. After they both got into the back seats, a driver with a bald and very scarred head wordlessly drove them to a nearby Italian bistro. Somehow, Mark was not surprised by any of this.

Steve escorted Mark into the bistro and walked through it as if he owned the place. With a barely perceptible nod from Steve, two men led them down a flight of stairs and into a special, private dining area that had been trimmed out with some very expensive looking marble and brasswork.

Mark had the impression that if Steve had given a different sort of nod, he would probably now be trying to tread water while wearing concrete shoes. He cleared his throat and asked, "Um, Bastille is a French name, isn't it?"

Steve gave him a look. "Yeah, what of it?"

"Nothing. Just curious. Nice place, this. Yours?"

"Nah, just some friends of mine."

Ever since he had met Steve Bastille as a freshman in college, Mark had never been able to clearly ascertain the details of his past, or for that matter, his true nationality. Steve claimed to be originally from Spain, but his name was evidently French, and his accent sounded like he had grown up as an Italian-American living in Brooklyn, although Steve had always claimed never to have seen the place. All Mark knew of his past was that he had returned to college as an adult because he had been dissatisfied with how his life had gone thus far.

"So, what happens now?" asked Mark. "You make me an offer I can't refuse?"

"Yeah, funny. First off, I need to know what you can do. You were studying to be, what? A dietician or something?"

"A metabolic biologist," replied Mark, smugly.

"What's the difference?"

"About four years and a hundred fifty grand," replied Mark.

"Fair enough. So, what kind of job do you want? What are you looking to do?"

"Well," said Mark while thinking, "I think my passion lies in trying to improve the efficiency of the human body. You know, like getting more energy from the same amount of food. Running faster and farther for longer, those sorts of things."

"So, in the context of a military subcontractor like AccelTech, you would be at home with something along the lines of making super warriors, that style of thing."

Mark frowned. "Well, no one is going to become a Wolverine or a Juggernaut, I'm sure, but I imagine I can improve their general strength and stamina. No problem there."

Steve thought about this. "Good. Good. Yes. I think that would be a good plan C. Yes. Fine. You definitely have a job. Welcome aboard." He wrote something on a piece of paper and slid it over to Mark.

Mark asked, "What do you mean by plan C?"

Steve said, "It's all very technical, but in layman's terms, plan C is what you use when plans A and B have gone tits-up. Look, my whole company is geared around my main project, my plan A. That's the project that got us the government funding. But you know me; I'm a realist. Sometimes things don't work out so good, hence my backup projects — plans B and C. So if everything goes to hell and the first two projects fail, we will all be counting on you to bring home the bacon. Hello? Mark?"

Mark was staring at the paper that had been slid to him earlier. He asked dreamily, "Steve, what's this really big number?"

Steve made a face like he was trying to play poker with a baby and answered, "That's your new salary of course, you chowder head. Oh, and your student loan... Pffft... it's gone. Forget about it."

Mark looked around the room as if trying to confirm that this was reality and not some dream. He asked, "You don't, by any chance, have any cotton candy, do you? I've been craving it all morning."

"What? No," replied Steve, sternly. "Look, this is serious. You're a good guy, don't get me wrong, but you're not so much better than any other guy, right? I'm doing this as a favor. I figure I owe you. After all, you are the one that gave me the idea for my new company."

Mark said, "You mentioned that earlier. What idea was that?"

Steve straightened up and his speech suddenly lost some of its usual mobster-like quality. "Do you remember that we used to sit next to each other in physics class?"

Mark nodded.

"Well, one day — and I don't know if you remember this or not — one day you started to make doodles in your notebook. You turned the corner of the notebook into a flip book by drawing slightly different pictures on each page so that when you flipped through the pages rapidly, it looked like the pictures were moving. If I recall, it was usually a picture of the teacher doing something unsavory with a piece of fruit." Steve cleared his throat.

Mark smiled. "Yes, I remember that. What of it?"

Steve continued, "I'm getting to it. So anyways, the next day, you flipped the book over and drew on the backside of each page. At that point, I think the idea was maybe starting to form in my head, but it wasn't until the following day that you blew my mind."

"What did I do?" asked Mark, interested.

"You started with a clean corner of the notebook. You started drawing pictures on each page just like before. But this time, you alternated between two completely different scenes. I think every other page was of Mrs. Birmingham dancing around like a fool, and the alternating pages were of people throwing fruit. I don't know what the deal was with you, Mrs. Birmingham, and fruit. That's for a competent psychiatrist to work out, I'm sure. But it doesn't change the fact that that was the defining moment when it hit me."

"What?" asked Mark, dutifully.

"My idea, stupid. Aren't you even listening? You see, Mrs. Birmingham was explaining that the universe is mostly composed of empty space. Even seemingly solid things are mostly empty space. Like, you know, all the space between the nucleus of an atom and its electrons is like the space between a fly in the center of a sports stadium and the gnats buzzing around the lights outside of it."

"Very graphic," observed Mark.

"Yes, well, while I was thinking about all of this, you nudged me on the shoulder and showed me your notebook. You flipped the pages and suddenly it looked like people were throwing fruit at Mrs. Birmingham while she was dodging it. I think you even did another one later with three different elements all going at once, each one on every third page. It was genius."

"Um, thanks," said Mark, confused.

"Don't you see? What if all that empty space isn't empty? Maybe that space is really taken up by other pages. Do you see? So right next to us, a gnat's hair away, could be a whole other world flicking by that we don't see. It's like, we are living in a world where Mrs. Birmingham dances all day, but on another page that we can't see, there is a crowd of people throwing fruit. So I began to wonder if there might be other pages / worlds / dimensions out there that we can't see? And if so, is it possible for us to view them? To travel to them? That is what AccelTech is all about."

"And you received government funding for this?" asked Mark, skeptically.

"Yeah, of course. Otherwise, we wouldn't be having this conversation. Mind you, I didn't pitch it to the brass in quite the same way. Mrs. Birmingham and her fruit did not come into play, if you know what I mean."

Mark laughed.

About that time, a fancily-dressed waiter served them their lunch, after which the two men resumed chatting. Steve slurped up some spaghetti and asked, "So, are you still dating that Lisa girl? Oh my god, the things I wanted to do to her. She had that sexy librarian kind of thing going, you know what I mean."

Mark blurted out, "We're engaged," in an effort to silence Steve before he said something that caused Mark to punch him in the head, which was an action unlikely to impress his new employer.

"Nice one," said Steve. "How did you manage that? You knock her up?"

Mark shook his head. "No, nothing like that. I just asked."

"And she said yes?" questioned Steve.

Mark shrugged. "Yes. Weird, I know."

"Amazing," said Steve. Then a thought struck him and he added, "Ah, I see. So that's what all this is about, this job hunting business. You're putting your big boy pants on, aren't you? Getting out there and becoming a man? Looking to be a rock that Lisa can lean on? That style of thing?"

Mark smiled. "Yes, that's about the size of it, Steve. And thanks. I really do appreciate the job. I'm not sure that I would have fit in at the other places, but I have a really good feeling about AccelTech."

Steve nodded and said, "Forget about it. Well, let's go, huh? I think we're done here." The two men stood up and shook hands. Mark did not know it then, but this single handshake represented the biggest turning point of his entire life.

CHAPTER 3

▼

"What's wrong with you today, Lisa?" asked Sharon in concern. "You aren't your usual chipper self."

Lisa opened the lid to the centrifuge and removed two test tubes that had been placed opposite each other for balance and frowned at them. She then turned her eyes toward Sharon as if noticing her for the first time and said, "Hmm? Did you say something?"

Sharon took the test tubes from Lisa's unresisting finger tips and placed them into a holder beside the centrifuge. She then linked arms with Lisa and guided her toward the door while saying, "Come on. I think your brain could use some chocolate."

They sat down together in the stillness of the after-hours cafeteria. After a while, Sharon prompted, "So, what's bothering you? Anyone can see you're distracted by something."

Lisa looked deep in thought as she pushed an uneaten and half melted chocolate bar around the table. She started to say something and then stopped herself. "I just..."

"You can tell me," prompted Sharon. "I'm your best girl, right?"

Lisa took some more time to think about the ramifications of saying something. Eventually she took a breath and gave in.

"Do you remember the ghost story that I told to you a couple of months back?" she asked.

"How could I forget it?" answered Sharon. "I nearly peed myself. I have to hand it to you; that was a great story. You have some imagination."

Lisa lifted her head and looked up at Sharon. She stared directly into her eyes and said, "It's true. Everything except the part where he was in the cafeteria with us. That was just fiction to get even with you for sneaking up behind me."

Sharon weighed her next words carefully. Should she go for the skeptical retort of, "Bull crap!" or perhaps another dissertation on the importance of keeping a scientific point of view? No, looking at Lisa's worried face, it might be best to humor her this time.

"Well, I won't lie and say that I totally believe that, but I can see that you believe it, so for now that is good enough for me. So... what about this ghost of yours? Is he bothering you now? Would you like me to steal some holy water from the church down the street? I'd do that for you. We could exorcise his butt back to wherever it is he came from."

Lisa shook her head. "No, you misunderstand. I..."

"You what? Go on."

"I don't want him gone."

"No? Why not?"

"Because..."

"Yes?"

"Because I... I think I love him."

CHAPTER 4

▼

The day after the job fair, Mark went to Lisa's parent's house to pick her up for a day of house hunting.

Lisa had been his childhood friend since grade school and they had been inseparable since the day they met. They were so close that some people found it creepy, and most of their friends thought of them as a single unit and dubbed them with the name of Lismark.

After meeting in grade school, Mark and Lisa had continued their friendship throughout high school where it eventually grew into a romance. As one might expect of any long-term relationship, they had gone through pockets of turbulence at the peak of their hormonally awkward phases, but they somehow managed to see it through.

When it had been time to go off to college, Mark followed Lisa to Stanford even though he had also been accepted to MIT and would have preferred to have gone there. However, being a gentleman, Mark never let Lisa know about this. Which was just as well, because, as it turned out, Mark ended up being very pleased with Stanford's biological curriculum and therefore never regretted his choice.

As for Lisa, she had two great passions in her life apart from Mark: chemistry and biology. Like Mark, she too had compromised when she majored in biology in order to be in more of Mark's classes, although she had secretly preferred chemistry. This was only a small concession, however, since chemistry and biology go hand-in-hand. Lisa had simply chosen chemistry as her minor and never looked back.

Today, Lisa and Mark were taking yet another important step together by searching for a house to call their home. To this end, Mark let himself into Lisa's parent's house and waved hello to them as he walked past the living room on his way up the stairs and on to Lisa's bedroom.

It says a lot about Mark and Lisa's relationship that this was entirely ordinary to Lisa's parents. Mark was like their adopted son, as Lisa was like an adopted daughter to Mark's parents. In fact, both their parents were also very close with each other and still lived as neighbors to this day. Mark once asked Lisa if she thought that their parents were swingers, but never brought it up again after seeing Lisa try to claw her own ears off in an effort to un-hear the question.

Mark poked his head into Lisa's bedroom and said, "Hey there, sexy momma. You ready to go?" He caught the pillow that was deftly thrown at his head.

Lisa blinked her weary eyes and said, "What kind of ungodly time do you call this?"

Mark looked at his watch. It was a few minutes past ten. "Um, late morning? Early afternoon?" he ventured.

Lisa shook her head and rubbed her eyes. "No, can't be afternoon, early or otherwise, on account of it having to be after noon to be afternoon — stands to reason. It's in the name. You miss these things if you don't pay attention. Good thing I'm here to work it out for you. Now be quiet and let me go back to bed."

Mark nodded and went back downstairs to talk to her parents. He knew Lisa well enough to know that she would be too excited to go back to bed and would be down and ready in a matter of minutes. This did, in fact, happen.

Some minutes later, Lisa sat down next to Mark at the counter that separated the kitchen from the living room. Lisa's mother was milling around in the kitchen.

Mark slid a bowl of cereal in front of Lisa, which she began eating without a word. She caught a certain look in her mother's eyes while she was chewing. She swallowed quickly, pointed her spoon at her mother, and said, "If you are about to say, 'Oh look at my precious little girl — all grown up now and moving out of the nest,' or any other such phrase, you can just knock it off right now."

"Oh, but it's true," replied her mother, and a tear started to form under one of her eyes. Then, to Lisa's embarrassment, her mother pulled a ragged tissue from under her sleeve and started dabbing at her eyes with one hand while waving at her face dramatically with the other.

Lisa looked down and covered her face with her hands while

shaking her head from side to side in an effort to erase this moment from her mind. Mark went over to Lisa's mother, gave her a one-armed hug, and said, "Don't worry, Mrs. Brabham, we aren't moving that far away, and I'm sure we will be around to visit all the time." This seemed to cheer her up.

Job done, Mark walked back to his seat. While walking behind Lisa, he whispered to her, "Don't feel bad. My mother straightened my tie and smoothed down my hair with her own spit yesterday. And my dad actually patted me on the butt." Lisa looked back at him in wide-eyed disbelief.

Lisa and Mark then hurriedly finished their breakfast and rushed out of the door before Mrs. Brabham became emotional again. Once they were out of the house with the door securely closed behind them, Lisa immediately said, "Let's just go somewhere far away. Far, far away. Maybe another country. I'd even settle for New Jersey."

"Oh my god," joked Mark, "Even New Jersey? You really are serious. Although I'm not sure it counts as another country."

"You've been there before, haven't you?" asked Lisa.

Mark nodded his head and made a face, acknowledging her point. He then said, "Well, she means well. She's just emotional. It's natural for parents to get emotional at times like this."

Lisa stopped walking, faced Mark, and said, "OK, maybe so, but see it from my point of view. All my life it has been, 'Oh dear, my baby girl made a doody in the toilet like a big girl,' and 'Oh my word, my baby girl just tied her shoes,' and 'Oh Lord above, my baby girl is off to school for the first time.' And always — always — she pulls an old tissue out of some cranny of her clothing and starts to dab at her eyes while fanning herself as if she were a character in some cheesy black-and-white movie. She only does it for attention, you know."

"My father says it's sexy," replied Mark, flatly. Lisa started scrabbling at her ears. Mark hurriedly said, "Joking! Joking! Only joking," while pulling her hands away from her head.

"Remind me again why I'm moving in with you?" asked Lisa with a smirk.

Mark smirked back. "Because no one else will have you — same as me."

Lisa nodded while swiveling herself into the passenger seat of Mark's rusty, old Honda. Mark got into the driver's seat and pulled out a printed map that was marked with the locations of potential homes.

Mark showed her the map and asked, "OK, where to first?"

Lisa's finger instantly pointed at the one farthest away. "We will start here and work our way back." Mark laughed and said OK.

The farthest house was a good hour and a half from their parents' houses. Mark used the time to tell Lisa about his new job, or at least, about the job fair and the interview that led to his new job, since he had not yet actually started to work there. When he came to the part about the signing bonus, he nearly swerved off the road from Lisa screaming out, "How much?"

Mark repeated himself. Lisa asked seriously, "You don't have to do anything sexual for that, do you? I mean, he's not like that, is he?"

Mark laughed and shook his head. "No, nothing sexual."

"Illegal?" suggested Lisa.

Mark shook his head again. "No, not illegal. It's government work. Secret spy stuff. Trying to invent the better mouse bomb. That kind of thing."

Lisa nodded sagely. "Ah, stuff that would be illegal if you or I did it, but since it is the government doing it, it's alright. And that money is basically hush-money to keep your big mouth shut about it all. Now I see."

"No," said Mark. "Well, yes, but not..." he trailed off.

"It's OK," said Lisa. "If you want to work for parasites, who am I to stop you?"

Mark repeated the bonus number and then told her his new salary.

Lisa said with humorous cheerfulness, "No, really, I'm OK with it. Long live Big Brother."

Lisa looked out of the side window for a moment and then turned back to Mark. "What will you be doing?" she asked before adding, "Or will you have to kill me if you tell me? Isn't that how it goes? I can just picture my mother now, 'Oh, my little girl is moving in with her first spy. Isn't this exciting?'"

Mark laughed. "No, I'm allowed to tell you about my work. They expect that we will do that much. But you really do have to keep the details secret — no joke."

Lisa creased her brow and asked, "So, what happens if I tell someone? Is it..." she made a slicing sound as she drew her hand across her neck.

"No," answered Mark. "From what I gather, they throw me in

jail for the rest of my life."

"Why you?" she asked.

"Because I would be the one who mistakenly trusted you with secret information. And because I was the one stupid enough to have signed a document to that effect."

"You did?" gasped Lisa.

"Afraid so," admitted Mark.

"So, what you are telling me is that if ever I get tired of you, all I have to do is tell someone about your work?"

Mark made a face. "I don't like the way your mind works, sometimes."

Lisa smiled. "My mind is sharp and flawless."

"Yes," agreed Mark, "that is exactly what I don't like about it. But that's OK. I knew you would think of something like that, so I took steps." He grinned.

"Steps?" asked Lisa.

"Oh yes, steps. In the event of my incarceration as a result of you having disclosed secret information, a certain lawyer has been instructed to deliver a collection of photos."

Lisa squinted at him. "Photos? What? Of us? You little pervert."

Mark shook his head. "No, not of us. I found them in my dad's bedroom..."

The car swerved as Mark tried to pull Lisa's hands away from her head again. "Kidding! Just kidding. No photos, I promise."

The car swerved yet again as Lisa's hands made for Mark's head.

Lucky for Mark, they had soon arrived at the first house so he was able to change the subject. Mark pointed to the house as they approached it.

"Oh that's lovely," Lisa enthused as they pulled in front of it. Only then did she and Mark see a group of neighborhood kids playing basketball in the neighbor's driveway. The banging of the ball and the screaming of the kids could be heard from inside the car with the windows up.

Lisa and Mark looked at each other and said in unison, "But it's not for us." They drove past.

Prospective home buyers often have lists of the attributes they would like to see in their new homes and neighborhoods, things like being close to shopping, a good school system, low taxes, etc. Lisa and Mark's list was a little different. It contained items such as: the house must have a north-facing bedroom so the sun will not shine into the room and wake up Lisa, the house must have a separate garage that will serve as a laboratory, the house must be near a hardware store, and above all, the house should be well away from noisy, little, bratty, kids.

Lisa made an "X" over their location on the map and instructed Mark on how to get to the next house. Once they were on their way, Mark asked, "So, how was work yesterday?"

She rolled her eyes. "You would not believe it. Hercules was in again."

"Oh god," said mark. "Is everyone alright?"

Hercules was a very large dog of indeterminate breed, but Lisa suspected that he was the result of the unholy union between a bull dog and a horse. Normal groomers would not touch him, so when it came time for getting his nails trimmed, his owner was forced to bring him to the veterinarians. As the veterinarians in question, Lisa and her staff would often need to resort to giving Hercules a tranquilizer before grooming him, but sometimes even this step was not enough.

Lisa frowned and replied, "Mary has a bruised rib, and I had to give Nancy three stitches on her arm."

"Holy hell," sympathized Mark. "What happened?"

"Well, after the tranquilizer took effect, Mary climbed on top of the beast to hold back its paws."

"This sounds bad already," interrupted Mark.

Lisa continued, "Nancy then bravely sat in front of the beast and began clipping its nails. She actually made it through a whole paw with no problems. Hercules was as mellow as a hippie on 'shrooms. That's probably why Nancy became a little too careless and clipped too much off of the next nail. She clipped a nerve, and the dog went ballistic."

"Oh no," said Mark.

"Oh yes," replied Lisa. "In an instant, Hercules swiped Nancy aside with one paw and ran. Unfortunately, Mary was still on top of him."

"Oh god, really?" asked Mark between laughs.

"Uh huh," replied Lisa. "But he bucked her off as they were going through the doorway. Bam! The door frame caught Mary in the ribs."

"Ouch," replied Mark. "So, what did you do then?" he asked.

"Well, I let Hercules calm down and then I gave him the real tranquilizer and clipped his nails myself." She smiled.

Mark took his eyes off the road for a second and glanced at

her. "Real tranquilizer?" he inquired.

"Yes, the first one was a placebo. I was running a test to see if the placebo effect worked on animals."

"Um, I'm guessing that's a big, fat no," chided Mark.

Lisa raised an eyebrow. "Really? You think so? It seemed like a partial success to me. After all, the last time anyone tried to cut his nails without first giving him a tranquilizer, Hercules had his jaws on her jugular before the other staff could stop him."

"What happened to her?" asked Mark in horror.

"Who?" asked Lisa.

"The girl with a mad dog gnawing on her neck. Who else?"

"Oh, her? She is fine. No more than a few days in the hospital. I think she works for a florist now. She had this irrational fear of dogs after that day. She didn't even come back for her last paycheck. Strange girl."

Mark glanced at Lisa again and continued to drive in silence.

The next house was even nicer than the first one. They glanced around at the neighborhood. No sign of kids. Good. They glanced around at the property. The house was astonishing. It sat alone on a hilltop and had the look of the type of place that only really important people could live in. The sort of place that is on tourist maps. The sort of place that, large salaries or not, they could never afford.

"Is this really within our price range?" asked Lisa in disbelief.

Mark checked the listing again. "Yes, surprisingly. It's even on the lower end of our range if you can believe it. It must be a typo."

"Must be," agreed Lisa. "Well, ring up the agent anyway. See if they are available now, since we are here."

Mark agreed and called the agent. After a brief exchange, he hung up the phone and said, "He's on his way."

"Cool," answered Lisa.

The agent arrived about ten minutes later. He pulled up in a red Mustang convertible and practically leapt out of the car before it had fully stopped. It seemed like only a second later he was in front of them with his hand jutting out for them to shake.

Mark shook his hand first, but truthfully all he really had to do was hold on. The agent's hand was doing enough shaking for the both of them.

"Hey. Hey there. How are you? I'm Thomas Weaver. Great to meet you. How are you?" said the agent. He sniffed his nose and then suddenly jerked around to look behind him as if he were worrying that he might have been pursued.

While Mark and Thomas made small talk, Lisa casually walked behind Thomas and caught Mark's attention. She then pushed one nostril closed with her finger while pretending to snort cocaine off of her hand. Mark saw this and nodded, then shrugged. Lisa returned to his side.

"Yeah, so, like, you two want to see the house, right?"

"That's why we're here," said Lisa with artificial sweetness.

"OK, OK, cool." He patted his pockets frantically and then ran back to his car. In the few seconds that he was away, there was a brief conversation between Lisa and Mark that went like this:

Mark: He's a nut job.

Lisa: People on drugs are easy to manipulate.

Mark: Agreed. We'll keep going.

They both nodded to each other.

Shortly thereafter, Thomas ran back from his car, dropped the key, scrabbled around in the grass for a few seconds, and then stood back in front of them with sweat on his forehead. He said rapidly, "Yeah, so, like, let's go, OK? Over here. Come on. Follow me."

Mark and Lisa looked at each other once again for reassurance and then followed him inside the house.

"OK, so, this is the kitchen, right? It's got, like, marble and stuff. You guys like marble? Good. Cool. And it's got all these stainless appliances, right? You guys like that. Stainless, it's good stuff. OK, so yeah, right, like, this is the living room. There's like, a projector up there and a big screen over there. Surround sound. Look, even a popcorn machine. You guys like movies, right? Of course. Who doesn't like movies? Movies are great. Now down the hall, there's the bathroom. It's a bathroom. Not really my thing, but people make a big deal about having a nice bathroom. This one is bigger than my living room, I don't mind admitting. Way too big for my tastes, but each to his own. And that hot tub. How many people do you think could fit in that number? Hey, have you guys ever seen *Hot Tub Time Machine*? Of course you have, you guys like movies, right? Good flick. So anyway, down here is the master bedroom. It is actually on the north side, which is unusual. I bet the designer was a night person like me. You guys are night people, I can tell. You're cool. Night people are cool. You guys like vampire movies? I just can't get into them. I mean, first of all, what is all this nonsense about pure-blood vampires? I mean, correct me if I'm wrong, but I thought vampires couldn't age. So if two vampires hook up and make a child, wouldn't it stay a baby forever? How's that supposed to work? I don't get it. Now come see the back yard. Here is the pool. It's one of those fancy infinity pools. Check it out. Get down here at water level. Come on, down here. Look. Check it out. Imagine relaxing in the pool. It looks like the water just goes over a cliff, doesn't it? And beyond it, there's the city, right? And beyond that is the ocean. If I lived here, I'd spend all my time here. Well, not all my time. Obviously I'd need to use that fancy bathroom sometimes, and I doubt that I would be able to sleep here, and of course I'd probably have to work a lot to afford it, but pretty much all the rest of the time I'd spend here. Yeah, pretty much. So anyway, if you look over there, there is that huge detached garage. It's cluttered up with equipment right now. I think the last owner was some sort of scientist. The place looks like a laboratory to me. All kinds of tools and stuff, too. Incidentally, there is a hardware store nearby if you need something while you're fixing up the place. I could have the garage cleared out for you guys if you want. It might not be safe for children to play there. Nah, you guys don't look like the children type. Well, don't worry, no little brats around here. Mostly busy urban professionals and movie stars here. No one that has any time for kids. Actually, over there is, um, what's-her-face's house. Oh, what was her name? Blonde. She was in that space movie? No? Well, anyway, she lives over there. You guys want to see the basement? There's like this whole fitness center down there. You look like you want to say something. Do you want to say something? Don't let me stop you. Go on."

It took Mark a second to remember that he had a voice. He cleared his throat while Thomas wiped sweat off of his forehead with his sleeve and then once again quickly looked over his shoulder.

Mark glanced at Lisa, who's every facial muscle was screaming, "Yes, yes, yes!"

Mark sniffed his nose. Then he scratched the back of his head. Finally, he said, "Not a bad place. Not bad at all. Definitely one to keep in mind. So, the price. Is this the actual price?" He showed Thomas the listing.

"Oh yes, that's the price. That's the price alright. Mind you, it's not firm. I'm sure I can get the seller to come down from that."

"Come down?" asked Lisa and Mark together.

Thomas looked at both of them and said, "Oh, that's a neat trick. Not creepy at all. No, not one bit. Yes, I think we could come down a little on the price." Something in their expressions was bothering him so he added, "Is that OK? You look... unhappy."

"What's the catch?" they both asked in unison again.

"OK, I lied, that really is creepy. Could you stop that now? Please? You're freaking me out here." He darted a look behind him again.

"Sorry," they said again at the same time, and then they both looked at each other and laughed. Mark said to Lisa, "I'll talk." She nodded while she continued to smirk.

Thomas looked worried. "Hey, you guys aren't like serial killers, are you? I've seen *Natural Born Killers*. That stuff is real. Look, I'm just a guy, right? No reason to..."

Mark quickly cut him off, "No, no. It's fine, Thomas. We aren't like that. It's just that we've known each other for pretty much our entire lives — that's all. She and I know each other so well that we tend to think alike. I could probably have a conversation with her even with her out of the room, that's how well I know her."

Thomas said, "No shit? That's pretty cool stuff, right? Cool stuff. So, like, what's she thinking right now?"

Mark looked at Lisa, grimaced, and then looked back at Thomas. "Um, well, I can't really tell you. It's one of those paradoxes, I'm afraid, like having to open a crate with the crowbar that is inside the crate. But in very general terms, she's thinking that I should do something properly or else there will be consequences."

Thomas looked at Lisa, who nodded.

Mark took a breath and said, "So, Thomas, between us men here, what's the catch? I mean, you know and I know that this place should be twice as much as the listing price, and here you are offering to go lower. So what's the jig?"

Lisa cleared her throat and gave Mark a look.

Thomas, who was weirdly perceptive, said, "No, no miss. No need for that. Your man just came out with it, and I can respect that. No one likes cunning little weasels, right? I know these things. I pay attention. I know people. I bet I could even tell you what you had for breakfast, miss. Cereal. Oh, don't look at me like that. No, I'm not a mind reader. I just know people. I'm perceptive. I pay attention to details. It's all about the details. And you have some milk on the corner of your mouth just there. No, the other side. So anyway, the catch. Right, the catch. Well the thing is, the actual thing is. Well, the thing is that there is a rumor that this place might be, well, you know, sort of slightly haunted."

Mark's smile faded slightly. He held up a finger to Thomas and said, "Could you just give as a moment to talk things over? We won't be long."

"Yeah, sure, OK, cool. Take all the time you want. I'll just be over here being bored. Take your time. No rush at all."

Mark turned his back to Thomas and went into a defensive huddle with Lisa. Lisa was the first to speak. "You know I hate ghosts. Better cockroaches than ghosts," she said.

Mark frowned and said, "I understand. I really do. I'm not keen on the idea either. But listen. Why don't we give it a try? Maybe the ghosts left with the previous owner. You never know. And besides... north-facing bedroom, garage filled with lab equipment, local hardware store, no bratty kids, fitness center, infinity pool..."

"OK, OK. Let's try it. If things don't work, I'm sure we can sell it for at least this much anyway."

Mark was going to hug her, but remembered just in time to keep his game face on. Instead, he looked depressed, turned around, and walked back to Thomas, who had been killing time by taking stones from around an ornamental shrub and skipping them across the infinity pool.

Mark made a face and said to him, "Look, I'm sorry, but my wife is not too keen on ghosts."

Thomas said, "Yeah, right, sure, of course. But you're going to take it anyway, aren't you? Because I'm coming down on the price another fifty grand."

Mark's eyes bulged and then he nodded slowly.

Thomas continued, "Good, great. It's a deal then. I'll have my girl send you the paperwork this afternoon."

Mark stood there and continued to slowly nod while he thought, this place, this glorious place, is ours? It just wasn't sinking in.

CHAPTER 5

Much to the dismay of many that knew them, Lisa and Mark had a very simple wedding ceremony at the county clerk's office. Mark also took the opportunity to renew his fishing license while he was there.

Many of their family and friends had been expecting some sort of grand event; however, both Mark and Lisa had felt that their marriage was something that was between them, and therefore saw no reason to waste a lot of time and money just to put on a show for everyone else.

In the end, only five people had attended their wedding, namely each of their parents and their common friend, Pryb, who had said, "I'll crash through the damn window if I have to, but I'm not missing my two oldest friends getting married."

The ceremony was short and to the point, but it still took some time to get through because every few minutes Lisa's mother would burst loudly into tears and exclaim, "Oh, my dear little girl is getting married," and then proceed to sob loudly and blow her nose into a very worn tissue that she kept in her sleeve.

Lisa chided her mother by saying, "Mother, if you don't stop interrupting, I may never actually get to be married."

After the wedding, the newlyweds flew to New Zealand for their honeymoon where they took a trip across the countryside on horseback.

Lisa's family had owned a couple of horses when she was younger, so she was at home with the beasts. Mark also had some tangential exposure to horses because of this, but he could never quite work up the same enthusiasm for them that Lisa could. Perhaps it had something to do with the way that the horses always seemed to prefer to chew his hair rather than to give him a ride.

The trip they had chosen was a guided tour through approximately one hundred miles of some of the prettiest country that God had ever assembled. They averaged a very poky ten miles per day, stopping often for meals or to take in the sights. They usually camped at night, but twice they happily found lodgings in one small town or another.

Mark and Lisa were not the only people taking the trip. There were two other couples in addition to the guide. Mark could sense them silently judging him the whole time. Everyone else had their own horses but he was sharing one with Lisa. This might not have been so bad had he not been sitting behind her the whole time with his arms wrapped tightly around her and his eyes firmly closed.

After the journey on horseback, they contemplated staying in New Zealand for another week. When Lisa brought this up, Mark said that his new boss was anxious for him to start so he really needed to get back. Lisa gave him a pouty face in return, which automatically gainsaid any further attempts at logic or reason.

In the end, Mark compromised by saying, "OK, let's stay another week, but I won't be able to help you unpack. I'll have to go straight into work when we get back." Lisa agreed with this in the firm knowledge that the pouty face could be utilized at that later date.

CHAPTER 6

---▼---

"Well, I'm off. Wish me luck," said Mark to Lisa as he opened the front door of their new home.

"Good luck," replied Lisa. "Don't mess up. I want to keep this house."

"Yes, yes. I love you too," replied Mark before giving her a kiss goodbye.

Lisa shut the door behind Mark and then walked to the garage in order to rummage through the lab equipment that had been left behind. Even though the majority of her clothes were still in boxes, she still wanted to start with the garage.

She began the cleaning process by picking up each piece of equipment, examining its condition, and then setting it down in groups with equipment of similar function or purpose. As she did so, she became increasingly aware that the equipment, when used a certain way, could be used to produce crystal methamphetamine as well as other similar narcotics. With this knowledge, she also took the added step of very thoroughly rinsing out all the glassware.

After a few hours, she grew bored with cleaning the garage and decided to explore the house. She walked upstairs and, on a whim, made her way to the farthest bedroom down the hall. The room felt like the loneliest and creepiest of all the rooms to Lisa, and it instantly made the hair on the back of her neck stand up.

In a way, this made her happy as it now gave her a chance to face her fears head-on and conquer them. But more than that, it also gave her an opportunity to study the phenomenon of ghosts. What were they? Were they the strong emotions left behind after a person passed away? Or were they something else entirely? This intrigued her greatly, and this cold, scientific curiosity also helped her to be less afraid.

Now intent on trying to actually attract a ghost's attention, she closed the door behind her. She walked over to the window and closed both the blinds and the curtains. It was now reasonably dark inside the room. She held her hands out in front of her and started to blindly shuffle around the room. She muttered to herself while doing this, "Here I am, a young, unprotected girl who is scared of the dark. All alone. In the dark. I hope there aren't any ghosts in here. Since I'm all alone. In the dark. Unprotected. Hello? Anyone? Anything? Hmm. Maybe it has to be night time."

She felt around the walls until she found the door. She opened it and tripped over a staircase. Cursing, she groped around and found the light switch. She had gone through the wrong door and was now in the stairwell leading up to the attic. She smiled and climbed the stairs.

Quite unfortunately, the attic was completely devoid of dusty old boxes containing either creepy old pictures, creepy old slides, or creepy old dolls. In fact, it was completely empty. She contemplated the idea of turning out the light to see what would happen, but her enthusiasm had already gotten bored and wandered off someplace else.

Feeling somewhat dejected, she returned to the garage laboratory and mixed together the contents of several unmarked jars of chemicals that had been left behind by the previous owner. To her disappointment, there was no satisfying explosion, no hiss of steam, not even an energetic blurp — just a muddy looking goop whose smell made her feel like she should lie down for a while. In retrospect, given the type of equipment that was present, she realized that this had probably been foolish. Still, it had been fun. She enjoyed being a veterinarian, but she often felt that in another life she really could have been an excellent mad scientist.

The chemical smell was genuinely making her feel ill so she sprawled out on the couch in the living room and stared blankly at the ceiling. What a boring day, she thought. No ghosts, no explosions, and no Mark. In truth, it was the lack of Mark that bothered her the most. Without him around, she felt like something vital was missing from her life.

This was not the kind of feeling that a person gets when they first fall in love and every waking moment is spent thinking of the other person — Lisa and Mark were well past that stage. No, this was not some whimsical love sickness. What Lisa was experiencing was more the sort of feeling that one might get if one stepped out of bed one morning and suddenly noticed that one's right leg had inexplicably gone missing. They didn't really notice it much when it was there, but they really, really missed it now that it was gone.

She asked herself why she felt this way now, since normally she would be at work at this time of day anyway, and not with Mark. In fact, maybe that was the answer right there. Normally she would be at work, but today she was home — their new home — yet she had been left alone while Mark started his new job.

It was not Mark's fault; she knew that, but the heart wants what the heart wants. And right now, Lisa's heart wanted to build a home with Mark — together. But Mark was not there. She thought about this. How could she make him really want to be home with her? And then the answer came to her.

CHAPTER 7

---▼---

Mark was pleased to learn that his commute to work was only thirty minutes long. His work was so close, in fact, that he could actually see it from his hilltop home. However, in this part of California, that did not necessarily translate into a quick ride to work.

Today, his first day of work, he had a choice between taking the freeway, which was notoriously stop-and-go, or taking the back streets, which were notoriously unpredictable because people tended to keep shifting around their routes in order to discover that magical path that no one else knew about. Sadly, once such a path was found, other people always discovered it too and the cycle kept repeating.

In the end, Mark decided to take the freeway because, although it was slow, it was at least reliably slow. He had even gone as far as making a test drive of that route the day before to note the duration. This was very scientific of Mark — some might even say a little obsessive-compulsive, but it proved not to be quite obsessive-compulsive enough in that a truly obsessive person would have done the test on a Monday, or better yet, over several Mondays, whereas Mark failed to consider that Mondays and Fridays tend to be busier than normal days, thus Mark was ten minutes late despite all his planning.

Mark noted with pride that he had an assigned spot in the parking lot. It was just a shame that it was in the back-left corner under a tree that was notoriously infested with incontinent birds. He assumed, correctly, that this was a sort of freshman initiation — a test one might say, to see how he would handle the situation.

Mark remembered that about Steve; he was the sort of man that liked testing people. He was the type of boss that would leave a hundred-dollar bill in your new desk to see if you would take it or turn it in. This was not to see if you were honest or not, but rather to see if you were stupid enough not to realize that it was a trap. After all, who misplaces hundred-dollar bills?

Mark made his way to the main entrance where he showed his badge to the security guard, who subjected it to the kind of scrutiny that airline personnel might show towards the suitcase of a Middle-Eastern alarm clock salesman. After several minutes of this, the guard begrudgingly let him pass.

When Mark first saw the inside of AccelTech, he had to admit that the place was not quite what he had expected. He had pictured gleaming white walls littered with stainless steel panels and important looking equipment that went "beep, beep, beep."

Instead, there was just a long hallway with pale green walls and a row of lockers lining one side. Lockers which, incidentally, were not stainless steel. In fact, most of them looked rather rusty. Mark found a locker with his name on it and looked inside briefly before continuing to explore the building.

While Mark had been busy looking around, Steve had sidled next to him and made a point of noisily clearing his throat and checking his watch. Mark, for his part, made a point of not noticing this. Steve sighed inwardly and thought, well, at least he is not two hours late like that damn test pilot is most days.

Steve put his arm back down and said, "Welcome to AccelTech, Mark. I see you've noticed the lockers. This used to be a private school for spoiled little rich kids, but thanks to the last stock market crash, I was able to pick it up for a steal. Well, that and I know a guy who knows a guy who is on the public planning board. But I digress. So, did you find your spot OK?"

Mark answered pleasantly, "Oh yes. Thanks a lot. That was awesome of you to give me an assigned spot. It looks like the lot fills up quickly."

"Yes, well, it pays to get here early," said Steve, trying to make his point again. This, however, passed unnoticed because Mark was now busy watching a girl who was roller skating down the hall.

Steve noticed this and said, "That's Roller Girl. I can't remember her real name — Dianne maybe. It's annoying, really. I mean, just because we are a Californian company, everyone thinks we should be another Apple or Google, like some sort of carefree think tank where otherwise perfectly sane adults act like spoiled brats. And none of them can take a hint, either. I mean, do I really have to make a policy forbidding the use of roller skates on premises? It wouldn't work anyway. The next day it would just be pogo sticks or unicycles. Actually, you know what I'm going to do? I'm going to get the janitor to really buff the floor tonight. I'm talking some serious wax." He made a gesture with his right hand as if he were personally applying the wax right then.

Mark, not caring about any of this, said dismissively, "Sounds good. So, any chance of you taking me on a tour?"

Steve sniffed reproachfully. "Yeah. Sure. We'll do that. And then we'll have lunch together. I have some ideas I'd like to bounce off of you."

"Alright," agreed Mark. He reached in his pocket and pulled out a hundred-dollar bill. He held it up for Steve to see and said, "I'll treat you to lunch this time. When I was checking out my locker, I discovered that some complete tit had left this behind. Can you believe that?" He furrowed his brow and added, "Or do you think we should return it to whomever used that locker before me?"

Steve smirked and said, "Nah, let's spend it. No one's used that locker yet. Probably some drug-dealing rich kid left it. It probably has residue all over it. I'd be careful with it if I were you. So anyway, follow me."

They walked together as Steve explained about the building. "As you can see, this here building is basically a big, hollow square, right? And it's got a courtyard in the middle, over there, see? This side of the building belongs to the bean counters, and the other three belong to each of the three projects."

They rounded the first bend and Steve made a gesture towards the old classrooms lining the next corridor. These belong to my Plan B. They're doing something with nanotech here. I'm told it's going to be the next big thing. Or, really small thing if you get my meaning. Anyways, I think the idea is to get the little buggers to work together to gather intelligence or something. I don't know. I never stick around long enough to find out. It makes my skin itch thinking about it, you know? Like there's these little things crawling all over me. Let's keep moving."

Mark, who had been silently nodding the whole time, subconsciously scratched his arm and nodded once again.

"The back of the building here belongs to Plan A. This is the focus of the company right now, like I said before. We call it the Flicker Project. Catchy name, right?" asked Steve.

"I like it," agreed Mark, who in all actuality was not very interested with it and would have been fine had it been called "Steve's Magical Wasteland of Taxpayer's Money."

"Would you like to take a peek?" asked Steve, hopefully.

"Yes, sounds great," lied Mark.

Mark noticed that unlike the wing for Plan B, all the doors leading to the Flicker Project had been replaced by windowless security doors. He also noticed that Steve had to have his eyes and fingerprints scanned as well as swiping his badge along a metal panel and entering a string of numbers and letters on a keypad in order to gain entry.

As if reading his mind, Steve explained as they walked through the door. "All security revolves around three things: something you know, something you have, and something you are. Low security requires just one of these, like a house key. It's a token, a thing that you have. It will work for anyone. Good security will use two of them. That's like your ATM card and pin number — something you have and something you know. We use all three here, plus I have two from the 'something you are' column, which is the hardest to duplicate, just to make it that much harder to circumvent."

"That's actually very impressive," replied Mark, genuinely interested now. "Is this the new location of the Federal Bullion Depository? Fort Knox was too well known, is that it?"

Steve laughed. "No, wise guy. And besides, I know a guy who worked there. There ain't no gold there anymore. We sold that off a long time ago." He tapped the side of his nose. "Just between you and me, capiche?"

Mark nodded and the two of them walked into the room. Most of the classrooms on this side of the building had been joined together into a single, large work center. To Mark's satisfaction, it had gleaming white walls with lots of stainless steel panels. Scientists with white lab coats and tablet computers scurried around while looking at things and making little tick marks on their tablets' screens. Clusters of tables laden with computers and lab equipment surrounded random prototypes of various parts of the project.

Mark definitely approved of this. He pointed with both hands and said, "Now see, this, this is what I'm talking about. This is how you make a lab."

Steve nodded. "Yeah, we went full-on geek sci-fi for this one." He pointed to a steel wall covered in blinking lights and added, "See that? Doesn't do a damn thing. Just for ambiance, right? But stuff like that is important. You can't have people like this sitting in a green room with rusty filing cabinets — they would simply wither away and die."

"That is actually very astute of you," said Mark, sucking up to his new boss.

Before Steve could answer, a man who Mark found instantly annoying walked up to Steve and said, "Hey there, Boss. Almost time for the big number. You want to look in on this one? Oh, hello there. My name is Brad."

Brad held out his hand for Mark to shake. Brad had a chiseled face, perfect teeth, and perfect hair that had been styled in that intentionally messy way that can only be achieved by spending several minutes in front of a mirror with a pound of hair gel.

Mark shook Brad's hand while trying to forget that up until recently his own hair had been styled with his mother's saliva. "Hello Brad. Nice to meet you. I'm Mark, head of Plan C."

"Really? Excellent," replied Brad. "The boss has always wanted a plan C. We'll have to meet up later and talk about it." He made a gesture behind him and added, "I can't really talk now, though. We've got this big deal going on. Our first big test. Hey, you want to watch? I'm about to test out the Flicker Camera."

Mark glanced at Steve for permission, but Steve was busy watching Roller Girl. She had just crashed into the superfluous light panel and was now waving her arms around frantically in an effort to regain her balance. Steve shook his head.

Mark turned back to Brad and shrugged. "Yes, sounds cool. What is a Flicker Camera?"

This time Brad glanced at Steve for permission. By now Steve was paying attention and nodded his head slightly. Brad saw this and took it as permission. He put one arm around Mark and started walking him towards the heart of the project.

"Ah, man, if this works, it is going to be pretty damn cool. Has, um, Steve told you anything about the project?"

Mark nodded. "Yes, a little. Something about other worlds superimposed, or interleaved I guess you could say, with ours. Other worlds that fill up the blank spaces. Something like that, right? I was actually the one who gave him the idea, you know? I used to make these flip books..."

"No way, bro!" interrupted Brad. "That was you?"

To Mark's embarrassment, Brad yelled out to the room at large, "Hey! Check it out, everyone. This is Flip Book Mark!"

Suddenly the whole room came shuffling over to shake Mark's hand and thank him for his contribution to science. Several of the team, especially the younger males, asked if he still had the original flip book containing images of Mrs. Birmingham and her fruit. Mark was forced to admit that he did not, which somehow felt as if he were admitting to misplacing a holy relic.

After the hoopla had died down and the team returned to their stations, Brad continued to explain. "Sorry about that, but I knew the guys would get a kick out of meeting you. We all get told the story of Steve's great discovery when we join, after all. So anyway, back to the project. Have you ever heard of the Simulation Hypothesis?"

Mark admitted that he had not.

Brad looked surprised and continued, "Well, it's basically like this: The whole universe is just a computer simulation, right? It's sort of like the Matrix, but not really. Unlike the Matrix, we don't actually have real bodies but are merely simulations running on a computer-like thing. I know, it sounds very tinfoil hat, but there are a number of scientists who take it very seriously and have found fairly substantial evidence in support of it." He looked around and added, "And most of them are in this room, so be careful of what you say next."

Mark said, "Yes, OK, I actually have heard of that before. It makes as much sense as anything else, I guess. I mean, millions of people believe that the father of a zombie carpenter just sort of made everything out of thin air, right? But what does that have to do with the Flicker Project?"

Brad pointed at Mark and said, "Right, right. It's like this: You know how a computer multitasks, right? It really doesn't — it simply bounces its time between tasks so fast that it appears to be doing many things at once. We think the Flicker World is like that. Our universe is just one of possibly millions of simulations running in parallel. At least, that is our working hypothesis."

At this point Mark interrupted and asked, "Yes, but if that were the case, wouldn't we move like this?" Marked moved his arms in a jerky approximation of stop-motion animation.

"Nah, bro. Not at all. Well, yes but not really. If you could watch us from the World Terminal, from the terminal of the computer running our simulation, then maybe you would notice a little, well, flicker — something akin to the refresh rate of a monitor. After all, moving pictures are just a series of still images shown really fast, right? But the thing is, we don't notice the time between refreshes at all because there is no time for us between refreshes. Our simulation has to be active for us to notice stuff, and it is only active during a refresh, but not in between.

Mark let this seep into his brain for a few seconds and said, "So, what you are saying is that we are only one of several million simulations running on some sort of cosmic computer and time only progresses for us when we have the computer's attention, the rest of the time is spent moving the other simulations forward. That actually somehow seems plausible. So I'm guessing this Flicker Camera is going to hopefully give us a peek at another simulation."

Brad lightly punched Mark's shoulder and said, "You got it, bro. Totally. Of course, we don't know what the other tasks are. We could be the only simulated world, after all. The other programs running on the computer might not be simulations at all. For all we know, we might stumble onto some kind of alien porn video. We just don't know. Exciting, isn't it?"

"Yes, seems pretty wild," admitted Mark.

Steve took this opportunity to interrupt their conversation. "Speaking of which, it's showtime. Brad, time to earn that big paycheck, right?"

Brad waved to Mark briefly and said, "Well, gotta go. See you on the other side, gentlemen."

Mark waved back but Steve only rolled his eyes.

Brad walked to the center of the room and made a show of stretching and taking a few deep breaths before entering a small room, or chamber, inside the main room.

The room looked something like a cage, or maybe more of a display case than a cage because it had clear walls rather than steel bars. It was a cylindrical room about 15 feet in diameter and was as tall as the ceiling. It looked to be made of clear plastic, probably polycarbonate, which is better known as bullet-proof glass. Inside the room was, well, a sort of camera that had dozens of wires extending from the back of it. The wires disappeared up into the ceiling somewhere. The camera itself was sitting on a pillar that also looked to be made of the same clear plastic as the cage.

Brad entered the room and an airtight door sealed behind him. He had enough air inside for a few hours before he would pass out. The door had several completely independent fail-safe systems that would presumably open the door before that happened.

The problem with completely independent fail-safe systems, reflected Mark, is that they were all usually installed by the same one guy that was habitually in a hurry to get the job done quickly and nip over to the local bar for a few beers before going home to his wife.

Brad, however, was a test pilot and therefore thought about none of this. Test pilots cannot afford to have an imagination. The key to true bravery was ignorance.

Mark leaned toward Steve and asked quietly, "So, how is this supposed to work?"

Steve thought for a moment and asked, "Do you know what a computer kernel is?"

"Yes, isn't that the main computer program that runs the show?"

"Right," replied Steve. "It manages all the resources for all the programs. It controls the CPU time and allocates the memory for the other programs that are running on the computer. And that's the key here. If you own the kernel, you own the computer."

Mark held up a hand. "Wait, are you saying that we are about to hack into reality?"

Steve gently waved his head left and right a few times while saying, "Ehhhh.... you could say that, yes. We think we can form a link to the next process in the queue, in other words, the next universe that gets updated after ours. As Brad says, though, we are just guessing that it is another universe. It could be anything. But we only know how our universe, our program, runs so we had to set up the link with the assumption that the data from the other process would resemble ours."

"And if it doesn't?" asked Mark.

"Eh, well then either we get garbage on the screen or... have you ever heard the term 'blue screen of death?'"

"Wait, what?" said Mark, genuinely worried. "Are you saying that if this goes wrong, we could crash reality? Is this what you are saying?"

"It will be fine, kid," said Steve, reassuringly, as he gestured around the room. "Look, white lab coats and blinky lights. We know our stuff."

Mark merely glanced at Steve and then back at the clear

plastic room. He then asked, "And what's the purpose of the bullet-proof, airtight room?"

Steve smirked and said, "Theater."

Mark looked back at Steve for an explanation.

"Look kid, Brad there is a test pilot. He's all full of macho... macho... macho-ness, right? When he's telling his grandkids about this day, he can't very well say, 'Yeah, so I just picked up the camera and waved it around for a minute and, well, that was pretty much it, really.' People like him need a sense of danger, you see? Anyways, shut up — he's about to turn it on."

The ON switch had a plastic cover over it that was painted with yellow and black stripes. Brad flipped up the cover to reveal a big, red button.

Steve turned to Mark and winked. Mark just shook his head.

Brad stared at the button for a long moment. He wiped a bead of sweat off of his forehead with his arm and winked at Roller Girl, who fell.

Steve saw this and thought to himself, wax. Lots of wax.

Brad started to count down from ten in a clear, loud voice that was being broadcast around the room from a microphone he wore on his shirt.

"Ten, nine, eight, seven, six, five, four, three, two, one, big red button... engaged."

There was a giant screen just above and to the left of the test pilot and his cage. All faces turned to it in expectation as it flickered into life.

The first image appeared, and once everyone had taken a few seconds to process what they were seeing, all heads quickly looked to where Brad was currently pointing the camera, which was to the right of the spectators and the opposite side of the room from the screen. Everyone then quickly turned back to the screen as Brad slowly panned the camera. Even Brad was watching the screen over his shoulder as he worked.

The screen appeared to be showing the contents of a room, a classroom to be more precise. Brad stopped panning for a moment and focused on a large whiteboard on which someone had written "Sally smells like fish" in red pen. The picture jiggled for a few seconds and then Brad stopped laughing and resumed his pan.

Mark turned to Steve and asked, "What do you make of that?"

"Well, I for one would stay away from Sally," Joked Steve.

Seeing the look that Mark gave him, he said more seriously, "I don't know for sure. The white coats will have to examine the data later. But just spit-balling here, I think maybe we are seeing the past. I'm pretty sure this is how the classroom looked before we moved in. I definitely remember that graffiti."

"The past?" questioned Mark.

"Or, a past," replied Steve. "Maybe that simulation was started later than ours so it is running behind. Maybe it's a different simulation entirely. We just don't know yet, but it is exciting, isn't it?"

Mark practically choked and said, "Very."

Steve smiled. "Anyways, let me go shake this guy's hand. It looks like he's coming out of his cage. Hang tight and I'll show you around Plan C when I'm done."

"Cool," replied Mark.

The crowd parted for Steve and graciously allowed him to be the first to congratulate Brad on a job well done. This he did, with the addition of a whispered warning not to instigate Roller Girl anymore.

Steve then walked back over to Mark, and the crowd instantly closed up behind him. They surrounded Brad just like a pack of wild groupies might surround a rock star at the pinnacle of his success.

Steve was now standing beside Mark near the door to the room. He put an arm on Mark's shoulder and said, "Come on. I'll show you to your new home."

Mark nodded and the two men made a left-hand turn out of the room. They walked around one more right-hand bend to the wing reserved for Plan C. Like the other three wings, this one had the same rusty lockers and institutional green walls whose color had been specifically researched by leading psychologists long ago to be the best one for turning young peoples' minds into tapioca pudding while simultaneously making them feel vaguely seasick.

This was OK with Mark. He had been expecting this. What he had not been expecting were the piles of construction debris which filled most of the hallway. Mark looked to Steve for an explanation.

Steve saw this and said, "What? We needed a place to put the rubble when we tore down the walls, OK? We'll clear it out for you. Don't you worry about it. Here, let me show you the rooms.

Steve opened the first door and flicked the light switch. There was a brief spark from inside the room and then it went dark again. Mark could hear water dripping and smell a strong scent of mildew emanating from the darkness beyond the doorway.

Steve quickly closed the door and said hurriedly, "This will be fixed by the end of the week, no problem. So, let's check on the next room. He cautiously opened the door to the next room and flicked the light switch. There was a double blink of light and then the room lit up brightly.

"There, you see," said Steve reassuringly, although he was not quite sure what he was trying to be reassuring about but felt it was important nonetheless.

Mark walked inside the room and looked around. It looked very much like the room he had just seen on a giant screen — a room that presumably existed in some parallel world, or if the theories were correct, some parallel computer simulation. This one even had graffiti on the white board just like the other room, although something different had been written here in blue pen. Mark read it aloud, "Thomas sniffs his mom's underwear."

Steve saw the graffiti and frowned, not so much in disapproval but in concentration. He scanned the room and located a pile of discarded white boards that had been stacked haphazardly in a back corner. He strode over to the pile and wordlessly began shifting through it. He gave each board a quick examination before tossing it aside for the next one until he finally found what he was looking for. He held it up for Mark's inspection.

There was graffiti on this board too — this time in red ink. Mark read it aloud, "Sally smells like fish."

Steve said, "Now that is what I call interesting. I'm pretty sure these were removed from the classrooms of Plan A."

Mark shook his head in puzzlement. "Curiouser and curiouser," he replied, a bit impishly.

Steve put down the whiteboard and said, "Yeah, pretty damn curious, I'd say. But it still doesn't tell us whether we just saw our past, or something else altogether.

Mark thought about this and answered, "Well, I'd say it is something else altogether if your hypothesis is correct — and it certainly appears so since the Flicker Camera actually works. After all, we are looking at another simulation running more or less in parallel with ours. But what is it of? It could be just like ours with only a few minor changes to the starting parameters which have since caused a ripple effect in which you never bought the school. Or it could be like ours only started at a later time, which would explain why it appeared to be our past. Hell, it could be something else entirely and they just got lazy and reused the models. You know how it is with programmers."

Mark suddenly started acting out the scene. "One of them probably called over his shoulder to his coworker, 'Hey, can I pinch that classroom you modeled the other day? You remember — the one on Earth version 6.2 beta. From that school in California.' 'What? You mean Sally smells like fish? That one?' 'Yeah, that's the one. So what do you say?' 'Well, I guess, but you owe me lunch.' 'Deal.'"

Steve gave Mark a hard look and said, "I've been on this Earth for some time now, Mark, and I have to say that, nine times out of ten, the most ludicrous answer is usually the correct one."

Mark nodded and replied, "Yes, probably, but perhaps some more tests might be in order."

"Of course. We just have to figure out what those tests should be. Well, when I say 'we', I mean the white coats. Something tells me, though, that you'll probably think of something too. But don't go wasting all your brain power on that because I want an outline of your project along with a rough budget on my desk by the end of the week. Capiche?"

Mark sighed. "Capiche."

CHAPTER 8

—————▼—————

Mark was slightly surprised to see Lisa waiting for him when he walked through the front door. She was wearing a blue lab coat that she had found in the garage and a big smile. "Wow. Hey there. Seeing me off in the morning and greeting me home in the evening. That's very Donna Reed of you. I'm not sure about the lab coat, though."

Lisa gave him a kiss and asked how his day had been. Mark replied, "Just about as odd as you could imagine. He looked at her in her lab coat and corrected himself, "Almost as odd as you could imagine."

Lisa replied, "Sounds interesting. You'll have to tell me all about it later, but first, there is something I want to show you."

"What's that?"

Lisa tugged open her lab coat with one quick motion.

Mark was motionless from shock for a second and then recovered nicely by saying, "I see. Very nice. Do you mind if I get a closer look, my little strumpet?"

In answer to this, she gently clasped his hand in hers and guided him up the stairs.

Lisa had always been of the opinion that being sexually active did not automatically make her a "naughty girl," and she despised it when men used derogatory words to describe her. The exception to this was the word "strumpet," which was a comical pet name that Mark sometimes used with her. Lisa let this one slide because it was a hilariously obscure word that sounded more like a type of pastry than anything demeaning.

Later that night, Mark started to play his favorite video game. It was a popular MMORPG, or massively multiplayer online role-playing game. He played it not so much for the game experience itself, but for the feeling of escape that it provided.

Whenever he played it, he felt as if he were taking a mini vacation to a different world. Here in this virtual world, he could forget about the real world and its complexities for a precious few hours each day.

The game also gave Mark the opportunity to chat with his friends, which he often found more enjoyable than talking with them in person because it gave him time to think of something witty to say and also enabled him to divide his attention among other things. He saw that his friend, Pryb, was online and opened up a chat window.

Pryb was the product of a tryst between a lawyer and an exotic dancer, and he had inherited cunning and street savvy from both of them. He was not a bad person in the same way that any given tiger was not a bad tiger. And like a tiger, Pryb sometimes metaphorically pounced on his unsuspecting prey and devoured them raw, but this was just his nature. You could no more blame him for such behavior than you could blame the ocean for drowning the occasional sailor.

One might wonder why (or how) such a disreputable person would end up being friends with the relatively meek lamb that is Mark. Their story begins in seventh grade.

Pryb had been unfortunately christened with the name "Stanley Przybylowski." Most parents never realize just how much a name shapes the person it attaches to. In the same way that a "Doreen" has an uphill battle not to become a secretary, Stanley had to fight against fate lest he became a tax accountant.

Had his family name been something reasonable, he might have been OK. With a little work, he might have even cultivated the nickname of "Stan the Man." But fate had something else in mind for him, because with a name like Stanley Przybylowski it was kill or be killed when it came to the other children in his school.

Before Pryb had met Mark, he had been traveling down the road to tax accountancy. The other children had taken to calling him "Slobowski" and had treated him with all the viciousness and cruelty that small children this age seem to have in excess.

However, all of this had ended very suddenly the day Pryb had met Mark. It had been an ordinary Tuesday afternoon. Pryb had just transferred into Mark's school a few days earlier after having been "awarded" to his mother in a rather nasty custody battle.

Unfortunately, it had looked as if the children of this school were not going to be any kinder to him. They were already surrounding him, jeering at him, and calling him names like "Slanley, Wanley, Pee-Pee-Lowski." Pryb had been handling himself well in that he had not started to cry yet, mostly because he had been thinking to himself that these kids had the mentality of third graders, which made him laugh inside.

Then along came Mark. Mark was not big. He was, in fact, very average in every way. He was not strong, but neither was he weak. He was neither handsome nor ugly. He was just Mark. However, Mark's bland exterior had been housing the mind of a very bold tactician.

Mark pushed through the circle of kids and stood beside Pryb. He said, not loudly but very firmly, "Leave him alone."

The biggest boy was just about to say something along the lines of, "Who's gonna make us?" but he only got as far as "Who" before Mark took one quick step forward. There was a loud SMACK. The kid went down.

Mark then asked if anyone else had anything to say. Before anyone had the chance to reply, Mark hit the second biggest kid just as hard. He also gave the first boy a kick in the ribs as a warning not to get up. He then said calmly, "Anyone else?"

The rest of the kids ran. They had just seen the two biggest kids in school go down like two dominoes in a hurricane.

Before Pryb could thank him, the teachers came running and hurriedly whisked Mark away to the principal's office where he was promptly suspended for a week.

Pryb had pleaded with the principal to let Mark off with a warning, but the principal had said that the school had a zero-tolerance policy against violence so Mark must be punished. This injustice made something snap in Pryb's head. He kicked the principal very hard in the shin and was promptly suspended as well.

Fate, however, had not yet finished pushing these two together. The next morning, Pryb stealthily crept past his mother who had fallen asleep on the living room couch after a hard night's work. He then quietly let himself outside and began exploring his new neighborhood.

Mark also went outside, but he was doing so to work down the long list of lawn and garden maintenance items that his father had assigned for him to do as punishment.

In reality, his parents had gone very easy on Mark. They were both secretly proud of Mark for standing up for that other boy, but they did not want to openly support the use of violence except in the case of self defense. Mark knew about their stance on violence and had tried to explain to them quite rationally that had he given the big kids a chance to make the first move then he would probably be in the hospital and self defense would have never had the opportunity to come into play. In short, it had been preemptive self defense. It was a good point, but one they did not buy.

Mark decided to start with mowing the lawn. He had the garage door open and was hunting around inside it for the gas can. He happened to be looking in the general direction of the street when he saw Pryb walking on the sidewalk with his head drooping down and his feet kicking at random stones. Mark called out to him.

Pryb's head jerked up and he saw Mark. His mouth dropped down in surprise. He then shook his head slightly and pulled himself together. He jogged up the driveway and immediately thanked Mark for the other day. He held out his hand for Mark to shake and said, "I swear, if ever you are in trouble, I will come down like vengeance itself on the bastard that is causing it."

Mark took his hand and shook it. He was about to make light of Pryb's remark, but the boy sounded so serious that he thought better of it. In the end, he simply introduced himself.

"I'm Mark."

Pryb hesitated for a moment and replied, "I'm Stanley."

Mark wrinkled his brow and said, "Stanley? You don't look like a Stanley."

"Thanks. I don't feel like a Stanley, either."

"What's your last name?"

Pryb hesitated again. "Przybylowski." He then spelled it with that singsong voice that a person uses when repeating something for the hundredth time in his life.

Mark thought about this. "I think I'll call you Pryb — P R Y B. That's a cool name. It sounds foreign. But I'm leaving out the silent Z — you don't want to be too foreign."

Pryb nodded and said, "I like it. Pryb it is."

From that day on, the relatively mild-mannered Stanley Przybylowski had learned to hit hard and hit first, thus transforming him by degrees into the formidable person he was today.

On the other hand, Mark, who had gained a ferociously loyal

friend and body guard, learned to soften up over the years since Pryb had cultivated enough cunning and guile for the two of them.

Now, years later, they were chatting back and forth with each other inside a video game. Below is a snippet of their chat log:

Mark: Yo. Sup?

Pryb: Same old. You?

Mark: Pretty much the coolest, craziest day of my life.

Pryb: That's nice. You seen that new alien movie yet?

Mark: Uh. no.

Pryb: Just messing with you. What happened today?

Mark: I can't really say.

Pryb: Ha ha.

Mark: No, really. I can't really say. My new work is mostly classified.

Pryb: Dude, that's like saying you know a really funny joke and then walking away. Seriously not cool.

Mark: Sorry. OK, well, let's see. Maybe I can tell you a little about work. I actually have an assigned parking spot.

Pryb: Oh, well, Mr. Bigshot. You probably won't want to associate with the likes of me anymore.

Mark: They gave me the farthest spot from the building under a tree full of birds.

Pryb: Totally messing with you.

Mark: Yes, that's what I thought.

Pryb: You going to let them?

Mark: Already got a plan.

Pryb: That's my boy. Any other riveting details you can share with me?

Mark: They tried leaving money for me in my locker to see if I was honest.

Pryb: What did you do?

Mark: I kept it and bought the owner lunch with it, making sure he knew where it came from.

Pryb: lol.

Mark: The place is a converted school. There are other projects there. We each have a separate wing. The other wings have been refurbished. My wing has all the construction debris and the roof leaks.

Pryb: Totally messing with you.

Mark: Eh, maybe. I think he just wasn't ready for me yet. Oh, that reminds me. Guess who my boss is?

Pryb: Donald Trump?

Mark: What? No. Steve Bastille.

Pryb: Steve Bestiality? From Physics?

Mark: Yep.

Pryb: Small world. Tell him he still owes me for that thing. He'll know what.

Mark: OK, next time he annoys me. So anyway, the main project there is pretty cool. It's straight-up sci-fi cool. I'm pretty sure we just discovered something today about the fundamental structure of the universe. Crap. Sorry. I'm teasing again. I can't really say any more.

Pryb: Yeah, well, I installed a marble counter top for the hottest girl today. I ain't saying what happened, though.

Mark: You got distracted and put it on the wrong wall.

Pryb: Dude, I hate you.

Mark: Yeah, well, you spend enough time with someone...

Pryb: Speaking of that, how's things with Nerdgirl?

Mark: Oh man. She stripped for me when I got home today :)

Pryb: Dude, I hate you. Just kidding. Enjoy it while it lasts.

Mark: What's that supposed to mean? We've been together for a long time already.

Pryb: Yeah, but now you're married. You'll see. Marriage does something to their heads.

Mark: This from a guy who never married and lives with his grandmother.

Pryb: She lives with me. Big difference, you bastard. Besides, I've got other friends. None of the married ones are happy about it.

Mark: I'm not worried. Me and Lisa are tight.

Pryb: There is a dirty joke there somewhere but lucky for you I'm a gentleman.

Mark: And on that note, I think I'm going to sign off now. Dinner is ready.

Pryb: OK. Peace out.

Mark: Peace.

CHAPTER 9

─────── ▼ ───────

Steve was sitting at the kitchen table and reading the newspaper in between sips of orange juice. His wife was cleaning up the morning dishes. She made a point of looking up at the large clock over the sink and said, "Honey, don't you think you should get going? You are going to be late."

Steve glanced up at the clock and said, "So what? Everyone else is late all the time. I swear, getting smart people to follow directions is like trying to herd kittens into a bathtub."

His wife frowned and said, "Yes, but, you should be setting a good example, shouldn't you?"

Steve shrugged and turned a page. His wife went back to doing the dishes, and Steve read the paper for another ten minutes or so.

His wife looked up at the clock again and cleared her throat. Steve closed the newspaper in a huff and said, "Alright, woman. Alright. Geez. You trying to get rid of me or something? You got a hot date I should know about?"

There was the briefest sign of panic on her face but she pulled herself together and said, "Funny. No, I just don't like to see you let yourself go. It's your own company and you can do what you like, I'm sure, but I just think that if you start going in ten minutes late now, then tomorrow it will be fifteen and then an hour and then down the road the company is falling apart."

Steve sighed. "You are right as always, my love." He set down the paper and gave her a kiss. "I'll see you tonight. Have a good day."

"I will. You too," she answered.

Steve gathered up his things and left for work. Five minutes later, there was a knock at the back door to the house. His wife opened the sliding glass door and let in a well-built man with a chiseled face.

Steve pulled into the parking lot of AccelTech about twenty minutes late. Annoyingly, some jerk had parked his crappy, rusty, old Honda in his spot. He thumped his steering wheel and sped to the back lot to look for a space. While he zigzagged through the rows of cars, he thought about his wife's shifty behavior and it made him that much more annoyed. When he realized that the only spot available was under a tree filled with incontinent birds, he thumped the steering wheel again in annoyance.

Then something suddenly occurred to him. He let out a short, loud laugh and said to himself, "Mark! Well played, you bastard."

He finished parking his car and took a long walk to the front of the building. He was working out in his head how he was going to deal with Mark as he flung open the doors to the building and strode in angrily. After two steps inside the hallway, both of his feet slipped out from under him and he landed on his back with a thud. His briefcase made a graceful arc in the air above him and landed heavily just beside his head.

He caught his breath and lifted himself onto his elbows, carefully monitoring his movements for signs of broken parts. He looked around him. Several people were lining the outskirts of the hallway and holding up makeshift cards with numbers on them. One of them said, "That's an average of six point five. Rather low, I'm afraid. Now, had the briefcase actually hit you in the head, well, I think you would be in silver territory. Maybe even gold."

Steve glared at all of them in turn and said, "Now, I know yous guys never seen me lose my temper, because if you had, you'd be running right now. But before I fire every last one of you clowns, does someone have an explanation for me?"

A member of Plan B carefully stepped forward and helped Steve up. He then explained that the janitor had apparently gone a little wild with the wax last night so they have all been having a bit of fun this morning watching people slip as they walked through the door.

"I see," said Steve. "And what happened to Roller Girl?" he asked.

As one, the crowd winced. The man from Plan B said, "Her legs sort of went like this." He held his hands straight out.

"I see," said Steve again. "Well, you clowns get back to

work. I'll have a word with the janitor. Oh, and if anyone sees the new guy, Mark, tell him that if he doesn't move his car in the next hour, I'm getting it towed away. Now go. Go, go, go. Go make science. Away with you."

CHAPTER 10

---▼---

Mark was in the AccelTech cafeteria, which was situated in the dead center of the administrative wing. Unlike the school children who occupied the building before them, the employees of AccelTech were not on a fixed lunch schedule. Since Mark was not tied to a set schedule, he decided to eat his lunch at an odd hour, which meant that only a handful of people were in the cafeteria with him. In fact, there were no cafeteria staff at this time either, only a solitary robotic arm that served the food. Amusingly, it still wore a hair net.

Mark sat down at an empty table and began to free his silverware and napkin from the plastic wrap that contained them. While he was doing this, a slightly chunky but not unattractive lady with reddish blonde hair (which was so thick that it would have been called a mane had it been atop a lion's head) set a tray down across from his and held out her hand.

"I'm Tammy Shaw — Head of Plan B." She tossed her head to the side so that one of her eyes was now able to see out from under her hair.

Marked looked up in surprise. Seeing her there, he quickly stood up. "Oh, hi there. I'm Mark Scottsdale — Head of Plan C."

Tammy shook his hand delicately and then said, "I'll trade you my milk for your pudding." She smiled and added, "Just kidding. Doesn't this place just make you feel like a kid again?"

Mark gave a polite laugh and looked around. "Yes, well, thankfully I think I'm too big to get stuffed into a locker nowadays."

Tammy gave Mark an uncomfortable appraisal from head to toe and replied, "You look like someone who could put up a pretty good fight. I doubt you would have a problem."

Mark saw where this was heading and decided to derail it by

saying, "Yes, well, my wife and I work out together all the time."

Tammy's visible eye instantly locked onto Mark's left hand where it spotted the wedding band. She flipped her hair the other way to let her other eye have a look at the ring as well.

Unabashedly, she said, "Oh hell, you're taken. Oh well. You mind if I sit here anyway? I promise I won't seduce you with my feminine wiles." She tossed her hair back the other way again and smiled.

"No, I don't mind. Have a seat."

Tammy opened her pudding and ate a spoonful while holding her hair away from her face with her free hand. She looked annoyed for a moment, dug around in her purse, produced a hair tie, and used it to wrangle a good eighty percent of her hair back into a ponytail.

"So, have you met any of the Flick Heads yet?" she asked between spoonfuls of pudding.

"I'm sorry, what?" asked Mark.

Tammy took a swig of chocolate milk and said, "The Flick Heads. You know, the jerks from Plan A."

Mark finished chewing a mouthful of sandwich and replied, "Oh, those guys. Yes, I met the test pilot, uh... Brad, and some of the white coats yesterday. They seemed like decent people."

Tammy looked a little disappointed at this, as if she were hoping Mark was going to say something mean about them. On a whim, Mark added, "Although Brad does remind me a little of Buzz Lightyear."

Tammy's visible eye suddenly looked over Mark's left shoulder and opened wide. Mark heard a voice call out from behind him, "To infinity and beyond!"

Mark's head sunk down and he shook it while saying, "Sorry. That really was not meant as a put down."

Brad walked around to the other side of the table and sat down next to Tammy. He said, "Pfft. Don't worry about it. I've been called worse." He looked at Tammy and added, "Isn't that right, beautiful?"

Tammy set her spoon down on her tray daintily and stood up. She shook her head to the side out of habit even though she was wearing a ponytail and said, "I have to go check on my work. Nice to meet you, Mark." Then she left.

Once Tammy was out of earshot, Brad asked Mark, "Did she hit on you?"

Mark nodded.

Brad smiled. "She doesn't care for me all that much. I tease her a lot, but I joke around with everyone. She takes it a little too personally, sometimes. She's a good girl though. Sharp as a tack. If she'd just ease up on the pudding a little and switch her conditioner, I think she'd really be a knockout."

Mark shrugged.

Brad noticed this and said, "Ah, you're pleading the fifth, eh? Smart man. Already stuck your foot in your mouth once today, is that it?"

Mark smirked. "Yes, sorry. So... how's the project?"

It was now Brad's turn to shrug. He fidgeted with his hands on the table while he answered, "Well, the white coats are having fun crunching the data we collected yesterday and arguing over their interpretations of what it all means. For me, well, this job consists of long periods of boredom punctuated with short bursts of excitement."

Brad looked around the room for a moment and continued, "I usually come in a few hours late on the slow days just to cut down on the boredom. Speaking of boredom, we all have to keep a log of our daily activities, did they tell you that?"

Mark nodded.

"Yeah, well, I'm a damn test pilot. What am I supposed to write about on days like today? OK, sure, if I happen to have an idea about the project then sure, I can write about that. But most days I just fill it up with stupid stuff just to annoy them. I don't think they actually read them, anyway. You know, I actually figured out the answers to half the problems they are having right now in trying to take the project to the next level, but I buried them inside an entry about my bowel movements and my strategies for World of Warcraft. They treat me like a dumb jock here, but I did go to MIT just like most of the other pinheads here. Hell, the boss man only went to Stanford. I bet I could outsmart that mafia goon any day of the week."

"I went to Stanford," said Mark without rancor.

"Really?" asked Brad in surprise. "Oh, yeah, that's right. You were Flip Book Mark. How could I have forgotten? Well, let me guess, you stayed here for a girl."

It was Mark's turn to be surprised. He squinted at Brad and replied, "Yes... How did you guess that?"

"I'm a people person. What can I say? That, and Steve told me a little about you this morning." He smirked.

Mark stopped squinting and picked up the salt from Brad's side of the table. He shook the shaker over his soup. The lid came off on the second shake. Brad laughed.

Mark said flatly, "No one actually likes practical jokers. Are you aware of that? Stuff like this is not funny, it is just being an ass. If you are OK with that, then so be it. But not with me, OK? I'll give you this one for the Buzz Lightyear comment, but if you do something like this to me again, I will smash every one of your fingers with a hammer." Mark smiled a manic grin.

"Dude," replied Brad. "Chill, bro. Just a bit of fun. Most people find it funny. You Stanford guys are real thugs, aren't you?"

Mark brought his smile down to a more normal degree and said, "No, they don't. Maybe some of them think it is funny when you do it to other people, but the problem with that is that sooner or later, it becomes their turn, and no one likes to have jokes played on them. No one. All you are doing is collecting people who dislike you. I think you are a cool guy, Brad, so please don't add me to that collection, OK?"

Brad audibly inhaled and exhaled. He tapped his fingers on the table a few times. Eventually, he said, "You know, you are the first one among all these weasels to push back at me. Even Steve. He lectures me to death but never really does anything. How did you become so ballsy?"

Mark scratched his cheek and said, "Probably because of my best friend. I've learned to handle difficult people myself because if I don't then he handles them for me. Have you ever heard of the Ultimate Fighting Championship?"

"He's one of those guys?" asked Brad, impressed.

Mark leaned forward and said quietly, "My friend glassed up the current champion in a bar fight last weekend because the guy was mad at me for eating the last of the peanuts."

"Damn. Seriously? Is he a Stanford man too?"

"You laugh," replied Mark, "but he actually is — although no one is exactly sure how he got in. He won't even tell me. He just grins and says, 'It's best if you don't know about it.'"

Brad held up both of his hands in surrender and said, "Dude, no tricks from me, bro. I promise."

Mark nodded and said, "Good. Then no hammer for you."

CHAPTER 11

---▼---

Mark trudged wearily through the front door and dropped onto the living room couch like a marionette whose strings had just been cut.

Lisa, who was also sitting on the couch, was bounced slightly and then tilted towards Mark. She let gravity do its work and leaned lightly on his shoulders. An arm slipped around him.

Lisa kissed him on the cheek and said, "I think I'm finally finished with the house. I put up the wall sconces along the hallway. Oh, and I finally hung the curtains up here in the living room. See." She gestured toward the new window dressings with her free arm.

"The house really looks nice, sweetie. I feel like an ass for not helping you. I'm really, really sorry that you had to do so much of it by yourself. It's just that I'm the project manager and we are building everything from scratch right now. We are on a pretty strict timeline too. Once we have a successful first demonstration then we can slow things down quite a bit and I'll be done with overtime, I promise. You know how it is, right? I can't rush things any faster. After all, I'm dealing with people's lives here. If I make a wrong move... god forbid I poison someone... or worse. Imagine a test subject drops dead. We'd have the whole facility shut down. The whole thing. You get that, don't you?"

Lisa put her free arm on his chest and said, "Yes, of course. I get it. Logically, I get it. But it still stinks. I can't pretend that I'm happy about it. I mean, even when you are home, your head is still at work. You know, I don't really need a big house like this. We can live in a small house and you can get a normal job. I mean, I haven't even found a single ghost in this crummy house."

"It's just for a few more months. After that, it will be great. I'll be home all the time. Things will settle down. We'll even go on vacation to celebrate. How's that?"

Lisa breathed deeply. "OK. I'll hang in there. Three more months. That's all you get."

Mark hugged Lisa and kissed her cheek. "God I love you. I never want to lose you. Just a few more months, I promise."

CHAPTER 12

─────────▼─────────

It had been a terribly long day at work and he and Lisa had just had another discussion about his job so Mark needed to escape the world for a little while. He turned on his computer and logged onto his favorite game. After playing it for about an hour, a small window popped up on his screen announcing that DeathMonkey was now online. He opened up a chat window.

Mark: Sup?

Pryb: You know, you would think a person would be happy with carpet in the kitchen. I mean, I had some extra and I thought, hell, she's cute, I'll do her a favor. But this chick, she sees it and she goes nuts. You would have thought I had just smacked her momma in front of her to hear this chick carry on. She was all like, it's gonna get wet and what if I spill food on it? I said, maybe you should learn to cook and you wouldn't have to worry about it. She made me take it out AND replace the linoleum underneath. No good deed goes unpunished, my friend.

Mark: I hear you man. Women, eh? Lisa's been giving me the sad eyes again. I know she doesn't mean it, but she makes me feel so guilty. I swear, if I'm not on the couch with her watching crappy TV every spare moment I have, she starts to mope around the house like a wilting flower. I feel bad, but what can I do?

Pryb: Damn, I'm sorry to hear that, man. Not to be a bastard but I did tell you this was going to happen. Something just goes BING in their heads after marriage.

Mark: Yeah, I don't know. I mean, she definitely has reason to complain. I am working a lot of OT. By the time I'm home, my head is spaghetti and I just want some quiet time for a little while. My project is shaping up, though. It shouldn't be too long now and we will be able to do our first real demonstration. Things will calm down after that.

Pryb: Cool dude. Well, hang in there my friend. I'm sure things will work out.

Mark: Thanks, bro. You too.

Pryb: Later.

Mark: Later.

CHAPTER 13

---▼---

Mark woke up feeling great. He slid out of bed carefully as to not wake Lisa and took a quick shower. As he lathered up his hair, he was surprised that he didn't feel more nervous. After all, today was the big day. It was finally time for his big demonstration.

On the other hand, he had been working like a dog for months now and he had certainly rehearsed the demo enough to feel confident that things would go well. Perhaps the prospect of finally being done with it all and finally being able to spend more time with Lisa outweighed any jitters he might have felt about the actual demonstration.

He finished his shower and quietly got dressed. Then he ate his breakfast and left the house early so he would have plenty of time for final preparations.

He was two steps out of the door when a voice said, "I thought we were going to do something for my birthday."

"Absolutely," answered Mark as he spun around. "This weekend. I have everything planned out. You're going to love it."

Lisa looked down. "But today is my birthday."

"I know, sweetie. I'm sorry, but today is the big day. We are doing our big demo today. There is no way I can't go to work today. I have to go."

Lisa looked back up, straight into Mark's eyes. "Please. I shouldn't have to beg you to be with me on my birthday. We are always together on my birthday. Always. Ever since we were little."

"I know, but maybe it's time to grow up a little, don't you think? Look, this is it. Today is the day. The last few months of me working my ass off and us not seeing enough of each other were all for this day. After today, we can have a life again."

"Yes, but why does it have to be today? You are the project manager. Can't you move it to tomorrow or next week?"

"No, I really can't. It took a lot of preparation to set up for today. We have people from the government flying in. It's a pretty big deal. I can't just blow it off or move it. I'm sorry."

Lisa was almost convinced but then she realized something. "You forgot, didn't you? I get that you can't move the date now, but you sure as hell could have chosen a different date for the demonstration than my birthday. You actually forgot that it was my birthday, didn't you? Didn't you?"

This time, Mark looked down. He exhaled audibly. "I'm sorry. I wasn't even thinking. Today just fit so perfectly with everyone else's schedules. By the time I realized it, it was too late to change it."

"Everyone's schedule but mine, that is. You actually forgot about me. We used to be practically one person, and now, you forgot about me." In between heavy sobbing she added, "I'm going home. I hope your test subject drops dead. I hope you drop dead too." She pushed past him and got into her car. She sat there for a minute while she dried her tears.

Mark felt queasy. He was so torn. He had to go to work. He had to. If he did not, he would absolutely lose his job. But something in the back of his head was telling him it was important to stop Lisa from leaving. He watched as she started to back down the driveway. His legs twitched as if he were about to run after her, but he decided against it at the last moment. He could talk to her later when she cooled down. After today, everything would be alright.

CHAPTER 14

---▼---

Mark stood nervously in front of a group of twenty-three very important people. Over half of them were from the government. Of them, half wanted to see if they could somehow weaponize his work while the other half was there to see that his work did not harm anyone. Mark was the only one who spotted the irony in this.

Just like with Plan A's space, most of Mark's area had been converted into a single, large space, the vast majority of which now featured an obstacle course. Mark's test subject, Rob, was standing next to him looking very fit and healthy. He had eaten Mark's special health food bar almost a half hour ago and did not show any outward signs of falling over dead, which was nice.

Mark cleared his throat and pointed to a large screen. He then said loudly and clearly to his audience, "I'd like everyone here to meet subject R. R has the physique of the typical enlisted man after basic training."

He pushed a button on a control he was holdng and the screen now showed footage of Rob running the course.

"We ran R through our course twice a day for the last two weeks to establish a baseline."

He pushed the button again. The screen now showed several graphs.

"As you can see, R's times have been up and down mildly, but he has made steady progress as he has learned the course. His first time was eight minutes, twenty-three seconds. His last time was seven minutes, thirty-two seconds. His last time was also his best, so we will be using that as the time to beat. You can see that for the last few days, his times have plateaued around this area. In short, he's hit his limit."

He pushed the button once again and the video showed a

tired, sweaty runner.

Mark continued, "No matter the training, every soldier hits his limits. There is only so much energy that can be delivered to the muscles, and soon the muscles drown in their own poisons and the soldier fatigues. Also, as the muscles work, mental clarity drops with the drop in spare glucose and other chemicals vital for proper brain function."

Another push of the button showed a rectangular slab of some sort of energy bar being consumed by Rob.

"We've developed a special type of health bar derived from all natural ingredients but selected and processed in such a way as to fix many of the body's natural energy extraction problems. R has consumed 42 grams of this mixture..." he glanced at his watch "...thirty-four minutes ago. Perfect. We have been monitoring his metabolism and know that he should be receiving the full effect of the meal right now."

He turned to Rob and asked, "How are you feeling? Are you ready to go?"

Everyone looked at Rob. His right leg was shaking with energy. A few people laughed quietly at this. Rob clapped his hands and answered, "Ready to go, sir. Feeling fine." He ran in place as demonstration.

Mark nodded and said, "Excellent. Then please take your position. Ready? OK. On your mark. Get set. Go!"

Mark hit the button again and the big screen showed camera footage of Rob as he progressed through the course. It also showed his time and his heart rate.

Everyone watched as Rob dove into a small pond, swam across, climbed up a rope, jumped over a gorge, dodged padded poles that swung randomly at him from all angles, stopped to read three math questions, ran through some tires, crawled through the mud, climbed a fence, ran across the top of another, and then at the very end of the course, he had to remember the three math questions and type the three answers into the console in the correct order. After he did this, his time stopped.

Twenty-three people plus Mark stared at the results on the screen.

Time to beat: 7:32

Current time: 6:04

These were not the type of people to clap, but they did so anyway. Marked smiled.

Rob walked back over to Mark's side. Mark shook his hand. "You were awesome out there," he said. "How do you feel?"

Rob was sweating heavily but his breathing was not labored. He smiled and said, "I have to say, I feel really good. I don't feel jittery, but I feel full of energy. I think I could even go back out there and do it again if I had too. That's good stuff you got there."

Mark shook his head. "No, don't do that." He pointed to a small sub-room and said, "I need you to go check in with the doc for a full physical. Your safety comes first." Rob nodded and walked over to the in-house medical center.

Many of the important men then gathered around Mark to both congratulate him and inquire about the next steps of his plan. In the middle of this, Steve's personal assistant gently pushed through the men and apologetically got Mark's attention. She pointed at a police officer who was standing at the door looking around.

Mark saw the officer and said, "Uh, OK. What's this about?" Doreen just shook her head and said, "You better go talk to him."

Mark excused himself and then reluctantly went over to see what the officer wanted. Mark had heard of the saying "The innocent have nothing to fear" but he had also heard the saying "Everyone is guilty of something." He wondered if this had something to do with the bar fight from a while back.

The officer walked him into the hall for some privacy. Not a good sign. After the door had closed, the officer said. "Mark, it's about your wife, Lisa. There's been an accident..."

The officer's voice started to grow distant. The corners of Marks eyes began to darken. He felt cold and hot at the same time. Then, suddenly, everything went dark.

Mark woke up in a bed of the medical center with the doctor and a worried-looking Rob staring down at him. He said in a quiet, raspy voice, "That was just a bad dream, right? Tell me it was a dream." When they both silently shook their heads at him, Mark's eyes filled with tears that quickly overflowed and ran down his cheeks where they soaked into his pillow. For the first time in his life, Mark truly wanted to die.

CHAPTER 15

───────────▼───────────

Mark was in bed, staring at the ceiling fan. Sometimes he had daydreams of it falling down and chopping off his head. Most of the time, however, he tried not to think about anything at all.

His hair was now straggly and overgrown. A thick beard had taken over his face since he stopped shaving weeks ago, and his body was now a good fifteen pounds lighter than it had been since before the accident.

Steve had kindly given him a month's leave to get his head right. Unfortunately, that time was almost up and Mark was far from OK. His life had been stripped of all desire. It was hard for him to even find the motivation to get out of bed every day. He stared at the ceiling fan some more and wondered what it would feel like to starve to death if he were to just lie there and wither away.

He heard the chime of his phone, which indicated a new text message. He ignored it. Staring at the ceiling again, he thought, why didn't I just go after her? What kind of bastard am I? I deserve to die. What is the point of me living? I can't think of a reason.

His phone rang. He ignored it. Minutes later, it rang again. He continued to ignore it. About thirty minutes went by and it rang a third time. Like the other times, he ignored it. A second after that, he heard the very distinct and very jarring sound of breaking glass from downstairs.

His heart started to pound and he sat up quickly. He started scanning his proximity for a weapon. He heard a pair of feet running up the stairs. He was frozen with fright and surprise, but he managed to grab something from his nightstand. A large man with a shaved head rushed into his room before Mark could stand up. The large man stopped a few feet from Mark and said, "What the hell are you going to do with that?" Mark was holding up a dirty soup bowl and contriving to look as menacing as he could with it.

Mark recognized the man and set down the bowl. He then said, "Jesus, Pryb, you scared the hell out of me. I can't believe you broke into my house."

"It was easy, too," replied Pryb. "Your alarm system is frankly a joke. My old granny could have gotten into here... with her walker. Anyway, I wouldn't have had to break in if you had just answered your phone. I thought maybe you were trying to off yourself." He looked at Mark's disheveled appearance and added, "It looks like you've been trying to do it by degrees, at any rate. Now, get the hell up and go shave and shower. I'll go find the least hairy things in the fridge and make something for us to eat. And don't even think of arguing or I'll throw you down the damn stairs. And don't even think that maybe that will be good because maybe you will die, because you won't — I'll see to that. It will just be very, very painful. Well? Get going."

Mark said nothing and walked like a zombie to the bathroom where he attempted to pull himself together. After he left the bathroom, the smell of Pryb's cooking wafted up from downstairs and made his stomach growl. Man, was he hungry. He shuffled downstairs.

Pryb had managed to make hamburgers and hash browns. They smelled unbelievably good to Mark. Pryb slid a plate over to him as he sat down at the table. He also poured him some coffee and said, "There you go, all the four food groups — meat, carbs, fat, and caffeine. Bon appétit."

Mark took a bite without saying a word. He ate half of his meal in silence and then finally said, "Dude, thanks. I am starting to feel a little bit better."

"Good," answered Pryb. "Glad to hear it. Now that we've got your body sorted out, let's see what we can do about your head."

"Oh god," answered Mark with a sigh. "Should I go lie down again for this?"

"You just sit there and finish your food," answered Pryb. "Uncle Pryb is gonna fix you right up. Now, first, tell me what is bothering you?"

Mark froze with the hamburger a few inches from his open mouth and gave Pryb a look that was full of daggers.

"You have to say it," said Pryb, a little more softly. "It's part of the process."

Mark put down the hamburger. He then said in a singsong voice, "My wife is dead, it's all my fault, and now I want to die. How's that?" He picked the hamburger back up and took an angry bite of it.

"I see," replied Pryb. "So you feel responsible."

"Of course I'm responsible," barked Mark, suddenly. "How many times did she plead with me to spend time with her? I kept pushing her off, and pushing her off. And then, like an idiot, I scheduled the damn demonstration on her birthday. Stupid! Do you know that we celebrated her birthday together every year since she was ten? Without fail. Until a month ago, that is. Look, thanks for trying to help but this isn't going to do it."

Pryb looked a little deflated. He said, "Look, I'm not going to tell you that you should forget about her and move on with your life. That won't ever happen. However, I can tell you that it will get a little easier every day. What's done is done. Constantly reliving it and beating yourself up about it isn't going to help. It's not like you have access to a time machine so all you can do is deal with the pain and move forward."

A hash brown fell from Mark's hands and landed back onto the plate. Mark suddenly sprang up and hugged Pryb, who stood there like a confused statue. Mark patted Pryb on the shoulder twice and ran up the stairs.

Pryb called out to his retreating back, "Hey, wait! Don't think you can run from me. You know you can't."

Mark answered back from the top of the stairs, "I'm not running away; I'm getting dressed and going to work. You just gave me an idea."

Pryb thought about this for a second and then shouted back, "Wait, what? You guys really do have a time machine?"

CHAPTER 16

---▼---

Later in the day following his revelation, Mark walked timidly into Steve's office. Steve's personal assistant, Doreen, was sitting at her desk just to the left of a closed door. Her desk was tidy, with only a few mementos on top of it. She only had one picture among them, which was of her cat.

Mark shook his head. Poor Doreen, he thought. Had you been called Tiffany or Ruby, your life might have been very different.

Doreen looked up from her computer and gave mark a smile. She straightened her glasses and said, "Mark! You're back. Sorry for your loss."

Don't tear up, don't tear up, don't tear up, he kept repeating to himself. It's a strange thing, he mused, that everyone keeps telling him that he needs to move on, but despite this, they kept bringing it up. How are you doing? How are you feeling? Sorry for your loss. Well, I was fine right up until you asked. Thank you for that.

That is what he was thinking, but what he actually said was, "Thank you. It's still very hard for me but I'm dealing with it. I think I'm at least OK enough to come back to work. I'm hoping it will help me to keep my mind off of things. Is Steve in?"

Doreen shook her head and her glasses went crooked again. "No, sorry. He's at a meeting with a supplier. He should be back around two. Do you want to schedule some time with him?"

"No, that's OK," replied Mark. "Just tell him I'm back to work. I'll talk to him whenever. I'm sure I'll see him around."

Doreen fixed her glasses again and said, "OK Mark. Nice seeing you again."

Mark gave her a little wave while turning around and saying, "You too, Doreen. Take care."

Mark walked out into the hallway and thought about his next

move. His soul was screaming at him to run to the Plan A wing and demand to be sent to the past, but his mind was saying no, it's time to calm down and think. He had to play it cool. He should act as normally as he could, and right now that meant going to his own wing and checking on his own project. After that, well, perhaps he would run into the test pilot, quite accidentally of course, and casually grill him for information.

Mark took a deep breath, cracked his stiff neck, and walked to the main laboratory space of the Plan C wing.

He entered the room only to have an arm shoot out in front of him, barring his way. The arm was attached to a scraggly looking man with a patchy beard and long hair pulled back into a pony tail. The man wore a white lab coat, or at least it had been white at one time but was now tinted with the same colors as the man's breakfast.

The man said, "Sorry, no outsiders — boss's rules."

Mark did not shout. In fact, he hardly reacted at all. He merely blinked twice at the man and said quietly, "I am the boss." Then in a slightly more accusing tone he added, "And who are you?"

"Mu...my name is Laslo," the man stammered in reply. "I'm sorry. I only started last week so I haven't had the chance to meet you yet."

Mark shook his head and put his hand on Laslo's shoulder while saying in a less threatening tone, "No, no, Laslo. You were right to stop me — that is the protocol after all. Even so, you are actually still messing something up right now." He frowned and added, "Majorly."

Laslo first looked worried, then puzzled, and finally enlightened. He snapped his fingers, pointed to Mark and said, "I.D. I need to see some I.D."

Mark smiled and produced his identification, which proved that he was indeed from this project and also the leader of it. Laslo studied it in detail, scanned it with some sort of device, and handed it back to Mark. He managed to say, "Welcome back, sir." He then stood mostly at attention while trying at the same time to vigorously brush off the remnants of his breakfast from his lab coat.

Mark studied him for a moment and then said, "At ease, Laslo. So, tell me, what is your job description?"

Laslo looked at his left sleeve as if the answer were written on it. After a few seconds of this, he answered, "This and that."

Mark raised an eyebrow, which was a move that he had practiced in the mirror several times before today for use on just such an occasion. He raised it ferociously now and asked, "Would you mind being more specific? Very, very specific."

Laslo looked nervous again and blurted out in rapid succession, "I Make the coffee, pick up the fast food or run to the cafeteria to get it, clean the dishes, stuff like that. Oh, and I handle the purchasing, some light computer maintenance — you know, like wiping down the screens and cleaning the lint and smudgy finger prints off the mice. Not real mice, mind you, the computer kind. And when I'm not doing that, they told me to guard the door."

Mark let this sink in. He rubbed the underside of his chin a few times with the back of his fingers while making a few logical leaps in his head. "You're related to Steve, aren't you?"

Laslo looked surprised. "Well, yes sir. His cousin, sir."

Mark patted him on the shoulder and said, "Keep up the good work, Laslo. I'm going to take a look around now. You can go back to... whatever."

"Yes, sir."

Now free to roam about, Mark took in the changes to the room. Things looked... fine. He was relieved, of course, that things had not spiraled out of control in his absence, but at the same time he felt a little... unnecessary.

Instead of one test subject, the project now appeared to have ten. Mark smiled at this and thought, it looks like we made it to the next stage of funding. Good, that means I still have a job and therefore still have time to gain access to the Flicker World project. Although, I still have to figure out how the heck I'm going to do that. Maybe I could talk to..."

"Excuse me, Mr. Scottsdale. Welcome back, sir."

Mark's attention sprung back from his daydream. His eyes moved from the wall they had been staring at to the woman that was addressing him.

She had red hair and a flattened face. She could have almost been called cute, but only in the same way that Pug dogs are cute. In fact, she had that same antsiness to her that small dogs often exhibit right after their master comes home from work. Mark just hoped that she wasn't going to piddle on his shoes or lick his face.

"Thanks Samantha..." he started.

"You can call me Sam."

Mark nodded. "OK. So, first off, well done for keeping things on track in my absence. I'm sorry to have put you in such a tough position like that."

Samantha shook her head vigorously while clinging to her tablet computer like a teddy bear. "Oh no, sir. Don't be sorry. After all you've been through... I'm sorry for your loss. If there is anything I can do..." she trailed off.

Mark quickly looked away. He had seen the hint of a tear or two building up in her eyes and he knew that if he saw her cry then he would start crying and she would cry harder and this would not be a good way to maintain respect from his people, especially after they've seen that he probably was not necessary. In a way, he felt like he was a Laslo — just someone that Steve had thrown a bone.

Samantha had an I.Q. well above normal but despite this social handicap she somehow still managed to notice Mark's discomfort and quickly changed the subject.

"It really was not hard at all, Mr. Scottsdale, to keep the project on track. Your notes were fantastic, and might I say, inspiring. I only had to follow your outline. Oh, the detail in your outline. It was riveting. I felt like I was reading a best-selling novel." She looked down and timidly added, "Just the same, it's better to have you here in person."

Samantha's face turned as red as her hair. Mark looked away again. Samantha moved a little closer to Mark and said very quietly, "Just between us, I let everyone believe that I was in contact with you this whole time, getting instruction from you. I'm sorry for the deception, sir, but I thought it would be best. This way, well I'm sure you get it, this way the team wouldn't forget who is really in charge. I wasn't sure how long you would be out, and..." she trailed off, as if she felt that maybe she had overstepped her bounds.

Mark quickly whispered back, "Samantha..."

"You can call me Sam."

"That was amazingly..." Mark searched for the best word "tactful — and possibly tactical — of you. I definitely owe you a favor. A big one. Thank you."

Samantha's antsy disposition returned. She looked to Mark like she was about to lick his face. Mark pulled back a little and asked her to bring him up to speed on the project. This, she flatly declined.

Seeing the puzzled look on his face, she stepped closer to

him again and quickly whispered, "I'll show you after work. You're supposed to be already up to speed, after all." She winked at him.

Mark looked surprised. He hadn't thought about that. Still, in the privacy of his head he secretly wondered if she had an ulterior motive. He treated her to a smile all the same and whispered back, "Thanks again. In that case, I'll make myself scarce until tonight. If anyone asks about me, just make something up. I have no doubt you can do that, Sam."

Samantha vibrated with self-importance. "No problem, Mr. Scottsdale."

Now free from Samantha, Mark left the lab for the cafeteria, pausing only to give Laslo a salute as he passed.

The cafeteria was empty and the workers were busy cleaning up after the breakfast rush and preparing for lunch. Mark bought a few things from the vending machine and found a cozy place to sit.

Huddled up in the back of the room, Mark chewed a potato chip thoughtfully while he tried to make sense of a world that refused to meet him halfway. Life had suddenly become way too complicated for him. It was hard for him to concentrate on the trivialities of daily life when the only thing that really mattered to him was getting to see Lisa again. It weighed on his mind like a Great Dane on the lap — it was heavy and took over all available space.

But in order to accomplish that admittedly impossible goal, he knew that he had to somehow keep it at bay. He had to metaphorically swat it with a newspaper and push it out of his mind so that he could concentrate on acting "normal" and not like the miserable wretch he really was.

Still, it was tough to think of a plan while all this other weirdness was going on. For instance, what was up with the girls here? What was up with Samantha? Did she like him? Was she just using him? She seemed like a sharp little thing. Manipulative too. Or was she just being kind? And then there was that flirtatious girl Tammy, although according to Brad that was just Tammy being Tammy and had little to do with him other than the fact that he was male. Even Steve's secretary, Doreen, seemed a little overly nice, but perhaps she was just being kind to him because of his loss. Yes, perhaps he was just over thinking things. That was it.

Mark looked down at his empty bag of chips and sighed. He

then stood up and bought another bag from the vending machine behind him. After he did so, he turned around to see Tammy sitting at his table. He nearly cursed out loud but managed to stop himself. Seriously — what was up with these women?

Tammy noticed Mark staring at her and said, "So, we meet here again. It must be fate. How are you do..."

"Yo! My man Mark. What's up brother?" shouted Brad after just entering the cafeteria.

Tammy huffed. "What's he doing here?" she asked, annoyed.

Mark smirked. "It must be fate."

Brad walked over and stood beside Mark while he said to Tammy, "Jesus, woman! The poor man's wife is barely decomposed and you're already hitting on him again? Give him a little time, would you?"

Tammy stood up and quickly turned around to hide her embarrassment. While fleeing for the door, she cried back at Brad, "You're such a jerk." She then put a hand in her jean's pocket and stealthily pulled out a small vial, the contents of which she discretely dumped onto the floor as she left the room.

After Tammy had gone, Mark turned to Brad and said, "Dude, that was a little harsh, don't you think?"

Brad said, "It's no less than what she deserves. The women here are like vultures. Haven't you noticed that?"

Mark said, "Yes, I have noticed that, but I was actually referring to your remark about my wife."

Brad looked puzzled for a second and then said, "Dude! Oh, dude. Sorry about that, man. I was just trying to get my point across to her. I meant no disrespect."

Mark stared at him for a moment and then decided to let it go. Instead, he asked, "So, what's up with the women here? They do seem a little... cougar-ish to me."

Brad smiled and answered, "Well, think about it. They are all smart chicks, right? They probably don't get out much, right? And normal guys, well, they say women have sex with their minds and men with their bodies. So here they are surrounded by dudes that can keep up with them intellectually. I suppose it's a turn-on for them. Speaking of which, you are going to really have to watch out for them now."

"Why is that?" asked Mark.

"Because you have that whole widower thing going on now. A woman's maternal instincts kick in around men like you. They all want to hold you and tell you that everything is going to be alright."

Mark considered this. "That doesn't sound all that bad, I have to admit."

Brad shook his head. "No, man, you don't want to go there, trust me. It's too soon. It will mess up your head. You'll feel guilty about it. No, take it from me, just keep your distance for a while."

Mark was starting to see Brad in a new light. Brad was a little coarse, but he did seem to have both a heart and a brain. Mark was starting to think that he could actually be friends with him.

Mark nodded to Brad and said, "Thanks for the advice. Seriously." He held out his hand for Brad to shake, which he did. Then the two sat down at the table and continued to chat.

Now that he was starting to consider Brad a friend, Mark was feeling a little guilty about using him to gain intelligence on the Flicker World project. A little guilt, however, was nothing in comparison to his desire to see Lisa again, so he started to press him for information.

"So, how's Plan A going these days?" he asked while bending down to scratch his ankle.

"Bug bite?" inquired Brad.

"Maybe," answered Mark. "Just an itch. Like something was crawling up my ankle."

Brad gave a short, quick laugh. "Probably Tammy. Everyone gets itchy around the Plan B guys. Lord knows what they are doing over there. Something to do with nanotech, but that doesn't really say much. Maybe they are making little fleas over there. I'd take a good, hot bath tonight if I were you. Maybe buy some flea and tick shampoo on your way home for good measure." He grinned.

Mark, determined not to be derailed, said, "That's weird. I'll have to ask Tammy about it someday. So anyway, back to Plan A, did the white coats learn anything new about the data that you gathered with the Flicker Camera?"

Brad looked excited and answered, "Oh yes, in fact, we used it a few more times and gathered more data, and now..." he trailed off and exhaled in apparent annoyance. "Dude, I'm real sorry bro, but I can't actually talk about it. The project has gone like uber secret."

Mark moved his hands apart, palms up, and said, "Hey, but I'm part of the same company, aren't I?"

Brad grimaced. "Yeah, sorry bro. Steve's rules. He figures

the fewer people who know what we are up to, the better. It's really cool stuff, too. I wish I could share it with you. I'll just say that with the Flicker Camera we were just looking, and now... now, we are about to take it to the next level."

Mark blurted out, "You mean you're going there?"

Brad looked around in a panic. "Dude, shhhh. Secret, remember?"

Mark covered his face with his hand. "Sorry. My mistake."

Brad replied, "It's OK. Just keep it to yourself, alright? Damn. I wish I could tell you about it. It's so cool." He looked thoughtful for a moment and then said, "You know we keep journals with all our thoughts on the project, right?"

"Yes, you mentioned before," answered Mark, dismissively. "What about it?"

"Nothing. Nothing at all," answered Brad with a wave of his hand. "Just thinking aloud."

Mark stared at him.

Brad then said, "You know Doreen? Steve's secretary? You should go talk to her sometime. She's a nice girl and has a surprising amount of... knowledge." He put a little emphasis on the word "knowledge." He then mumbled half to himself, "or at least access to knowledge."

Mark looked confused. "I thought you said I should stay away from the women here for a while?"

"Did I?" asked Brad, impishly. "Oh, yes, of course. It was just a thought. Do with it what you will."

Brad then suddenly looked at his watch and stood up. "Well, it's been fun but I have to go. Nice having you around the place again, Mark. Give a little thought to what I just said." He gave Mark a backwards wave and was out of the door before Mark could even respond.

"What the heck was that all about?" he asked himself aloud. He scratched his ankle again mindlessly and then left the building to take a walk and kill some time before he could return to his project once everyone but Samantha had gone home. That should be fun, he reflected.

CHAPTER 17

---▼---

Tammy quickly scurried to the other side of the building and returned to the Plan B wing. She practically dove into her personal office and slammed the door behind her.

Her chair creaked menacingly as she threw herself into it with a huff. "Stupid Brad," she muttered to herself as she turned her attention to a video screen and a set of complex controls. She flicked a switch with a flourish and said to herself, "OK, we have video."

The screen was now showing video of the cafeteria, taken from ground level. The video was of low resolution, but it was clear enough to use for navigation. Tammy used the controls to move the camera towards Mark.

Tammy moved the controls and a swarm of tiny particles no bigger than motes of dust moved in unison. Each one had exactly one light sensor, but since there were thousands of them, they could work together to form a crude black and white camera.

The camera was only two feet from Mark when both Mark and Brad suddenly walked over to a nearby table and sat down. The video went momentarily blank as Brad stepped on it.

"Stupid Brad," she repeated and then turned the camera around.

She then steered the camera to within a few inches of Mark's left foot and said to herself, "Target acquired. Deploying audio."

Two specks of dust broke off from the group and traveled to Marks shoe. Tammy could not see them on her screen, but she could guide them to the target using a cursor on the screen. They would report back when they were in position.

While the audio bugs were in transit, Tammy wrangled her hair into a pony tail and then put on a pair of headphones.

A green light lit up next to the words "Audio Ready." Tammy

flipped a switch and then jumped at the amplified sound of Mark scratching his ankle.

She momentarily pulled the headphones off and then cautiously put them back on. She then listened intently for about a minute before she said, "So, we make them itch, do we? Hmm. Maybe we can coat the mites with a local anesthetic? We'll have to work on that."

After another few minutes of listening, she said, "Why all the interest in the Flicker project, Mark? You a spy? Up to no good? You're a bad, bad, boy, Mark. I may have to discipline you."

Another few minutes passed and once again she said to herself, "What's this about Doreen? You can't take a hint to save your life, can you Mark? I wonder what that stupid test pilot knows? Let's find out. Deploying audio."

Two more mites broke off from the main cluster and slowly made their way towards Brad. Unfortunately for both the mites and Tammy, Brad suddenly stood up and left the room before they got to him.

Tammy cursed under her breath and took the headphones off in a huff. She removed the band holding back her hair and shook it out. With a smile she said, "Well, at least I have Mark."

CHAPTER 18

---▼---

Mark had spent part of the day walking around AccelTech's neighborhood until he grew tired and returned home to kill time playing video games until five o'clock, at which point he would have to meet with Samantha after hours. He was not looking forward to it and had a really bad feeling about her.

While he was playing his game, he suddenly received a chat request from Pryb. He paused the game and opened the chat window.

Mark: Yo. Sup?

Pryb: Dude, first day back at work and you are already playing hooky? Not good.

Mark: LOL. No, it's not like that. Well, yes it is but not really. It's a long story but the general gist is that my assistant, Samantha, was nice enough (or crafty enough) to pretend to be taking direction from me this whole time. She wants to get me up to speed on the project after hours so I don't look clueless in front of the others.

Pryb: Sounds like a scam. Is she hot?

Mark: Do you like Pug dogs?

Pryb: Smooshy faced, huh?

Mark: Yes. Sort of cute, I suppose, but only in a weird way.

Pryb: I got ya. Anyway, stay alert. At best she is just trying to hit on you. Maybe she has your best interest in mind, but I wouldn't count on it.

Mark: Yes, thanks, that's what I thought too.

Pryb: Anything else going on?

Mark: Yes. I talked to the test pilot today. It looks like the Flicker World project has gone top secret. He couldn't even talk about it with me. He did seem like he was trying to tell me something at the end of our conversation, though, but it made no sense.

Pryb: What did he say?

Mark: First he suddenly brought up the fact that everyone records their thoughts into a journal that is stored on the central computer, which is odd because he knows I know that. Then he started to ramble on about Steve's secretary. I don't know what to make of it.

Pryb: Dude, you're clueless. Everyone knows that the secretary of the boss has the most access of anyone in the company, including the boss. Secretarial assistants do EVERYTHING. I think you should listen to the pilot and take an interest in her. Find out what she likes. What are her hobbies? The names of her pets, her children, those sorts of things.

Mark: Why?

Pryb: <facepalm> Dude, to find out her password so we can read the test pilot's journal. Are you brain dead?

Mark: Ooooooh! LOL, yes I'm brain dead. Thanks, I'll do that. Crap, I have to go, it's nearly 4:30.

Pryb: OK then. Later, bro. Enjoy your date.

Mark: Not funny, dude. Later.

CHAPTER 19

▼

Mark held his breath as he entered the main lab area of Plan C. He had half expected the place to be moodily lit but it was not, nor was Samantha scantily dressed. In fact, she was wearing her usual white lab coat. Mark briefly flashed back to when Lisa had torn off her lab coat for him as a very special welcome home. This briefly excited him, and then it made him completely miserable.

Samantha noticed the pained expression on his face and said, "Are you alright, sir? This won't take long, I promise."

Mark's attention snapped back to the present. He stared blankly at Samantha for a second and shook his head. "Sorry, no, I was just spacing out. I have a lot on my mind. Anyway, thanks again for doing this for me. I feel like such a heel."

Samantha slightly shook her head and said, "No, don't worry about it. I completely understand. How about we just dive into things, shall we?"

"OK," agreed Mark.

Samantha began walking him around the lab. As they walked, she said, "So, I'm sure you noticed that we have more test subjects now. We met our funding goals thanks to your brilliant demonstration last month. I think the brass at the Department of Defense had a quiet chat to the guys from the Food and Drug Administration and explained to them the benefits of keeping an open mind towards human experimentation. I think as long as we don't actually kill anyone, we won't be seeing them around here anymore."

Mark gave her a worried half smile and said, "Good. That's good."

Samantha walked him over to the obstacle course and said, "We've installed low power laser beams before and after each of the obstacles now so we can measure the subject's time for each element individually. I thought it might be interesting to know exactly which activities our subjects are improving at the most, and perhaps see if there were any in which they actually declined."

Mark studied the additions and said, "That was a fantastic idea, Samantha. It never hurts to have more data."

"Thank you sir," replied Samantha. She was visibly pleased to have been praised.

Mark asked, "What about the actual research material? Have you been trying out variations of the formula to determine the optimal ratios?"

Samantha nodded and replied while typing on her tablet computer, "Yes, of course. Just like your plan specified, we are varying the ingredients by plus and minus twenty percent in every conceivable combination." She finished typing and passed the tablet to Mark.

Mark studied the test plan for some time and said, "Yes, looks like you've got it covered perfectly. I see you are also introducing some new ingredients into some of the combinations. You don't think it's a little late in the game to be changing the formula?"

Samantha delicately took the tablet back from Mark and began typing on it again while saying, "No, not really, sir. I mean, there is always room for improvement, am I right? That's what we are here to do, yes? If we eek out a few percentages of improvement from combining several strategies, then before we know it, we've made some really big leaps. My thoughts are that the more strategies we employ, the better."

Mark said, "Agreed. I just don't want us to have too many balls in the air and lose track of them all. Too many variables can also start to work against one another. I've always been a proponent of the KISS method. You know, Keep It Simple, Stupid — not that I'm calling you stupid, of course."

"Understood, sir. She handed him the tablet again and said, "But you can see here in the samples in which we've introduced L-lysine in a matrix of beta-carotene, there seems to be a slight but consistent improvement."

Mark said, "Mmm... yummy. Now I could really go for a hot bowl of stew."

"I'm sorry, sir?" questioned Samantha. Her flat face wrinkled up slightly.

"Beef and carrots," prompted Mark.

After seeing the continued blank expression on her face, he added, "The dietary sources of those two compounds are mainly beef and carrots, so... stew. Sorry, I guess I'm just getting hungry and my mind is wandering. Please continue."

"Oh, yes, I see it now sir. Very funny," replied Samantha, who was not even smiling let alone laughing.

Mark studied the tablet to hide his embarrassment and said, "At any rate, it seems like a good call so far. Up to a three percent increase in stamina, it seems."

Samantha brightened up again. "Yes, well spotted, sir. We mirrored some of the tests at the beginning and end of the course so we can get a better idea of the subject's rate of fatigue."

Mark asked, "What kind of side effects have we noted so far?"

Samantha took back the tablet, typed on it for a moment, and then read the list of potential side effects, "Headaches, fever, sleeplessness, nausea, stomach aches, diarrhea, body odor, bad luck, and pregnancy."

"Bad luck and pregnancy?" questioned Mark.

Samantha shrugged. "We have to write down all complaints, rational or not."

Mark asked, "So how many of those are demonstratively repeatable?"

"Only the body odor, sir."

"Yes, well," said Mark, "they are running around all day covered in sweat, after all."

"True, sir," Samantha admitted, "but we still have to write it down."

"Granted," Mark conceded. "So, anything else you need to show me?"

Samantha checked her tablet. "No... I guess that about wraps it up for tonight. You can review the notes in the system to fill in any of the other details."

Mark thought to himself, "Well, it looks like my fears were unfounded. At least it's clear that she isn't trying to seduce me. Against all odds, she just might be a normal person who is sincerely trying to do her job to the best of her ability. Maybe we should stuff her and keep her preserved on a shelf like some rare and treasured specimen."

"Sir?"

"Yes? Hello? What?" said Mark, startled out of deep thought.

"You were staring at me funny. Is anything wrong?"

"No, no. Sorry. I think I'm just spacing out from hunger. Do you want to go grab a bite to eat? My treat for keeping you out so late."

Samantha's face turned red. She clutched her tablet to her chest in much the same way that an exorcist might cling to the Bible. She then stammered out an excuse and hurriedly left the room.

Mark cursed. He really had not meant anything by the dinner invitation, but clearly she had taken it the wrong way. He had just been feeling hungry and stupidly thought that it would only be polite to offer to feed her since she would presumably be hungry as well.

Mark asked himself, "What am I? You are an idiot. A complete and total nitwit."

Meanwhile, on the other side of the building, Tammy pulled off her headphones and said, "Yes you are, Mark. Yes you are."

CHAPTER 20

▼

"Oh my, Mark. How nice to see you," said Doreen while sitting to attention and endeavoring to straighten her glasses, which fell slightly crooked not two seconds later.

"Doreen, hi, how are you? Is the big guy around?" asked Mark, who already knew the answer since he had just watched Steve walk out of the main door not five minutes earlier.

Doreen shook her head and said, "No, sorry. You've just missed him. He's on his way to meet with the government again. They are very adamant about being kept current on the research of all three projects. It seems that now that they've funded us, they think they own us." She snorted as if she had just said something incredibly funny.

Mark gave a hollow laugh and said, "The nerve of them, right?"

"Indeed," replied Doreen.

The conversation lulled for a moment while Mark thought about what to say next. He saw the cat picture and asked, "Oh, is that your cat? What's his name?"

Doreen brightened up as if Mark were asking about the most important thing in her life, which sadly, he was. She looked at the picture and said, "His real name is Stanley, but I just call him Fuzzybutt." She snorted again in shear comedic ecstasy.

"Fuzzybutt?" confirmed Mark. "Very cute. So, um, what else do you do when you're not spending time with Fuzzybutt? Do you have any hobbies?"

"Me?" asked Doreen, who was not used to personal questions from the opposite sex. "Oh, I don't know. Not much, really. Although I do enjoy a good bingo game on Sunday nights. The ladies and I meet up at Saint Stephan's and play a few games after mass. It's great fun. You should come sometime."

Mark rubbed the back of his neck and said, "Yes, ha-ha, maybe I will sometime. Sounds fun. So... How about TV shows? Do you watch TV?"

"Sometimes," admitted Doreen.

"Any favorites?" prompted Mark.

"I do like to watch reruns of Sex and the City," she admitted.

Mark nearly choked. A large part of his brain was yelling at his mouth to change the topic.

Mark said, "Ah, yes. My Lisa used to watch that too. I could never get into it, myself. So, um, apart from bingo on Sunday nights, do you belong to any other groups?"

"Well," said Doreen, "actually, there is the crocheting club on Tuesday nights..."

"That's nice," interjected Mark.

"...and the lesbian support group that meets every other Thursday."

Mark looked momentarily shocked until he realized that she must be joking. He waited for the tell-tale snort, only it never came.

Despite a major part of his brain jumping up and down while telling his mouth to change the subject again, he heard his own voice ask, "Oh wow, so you're a lesbian?"

Doreen straightened her glasses and said, "Oh, well, I don't know about that. I'm just curious, really."

Mark's mouth finally got the hint and said, "Ah, well, that's perfectly natural. So, um, art... how about art? Any favorite artists?"

Doreen thought about this and answered, "I guess I'd have to say Salvador Dali."

Mark wrinkled his forehead and asked, "Which one was he? Wait, I know, the one with the crazy mustache and the paintings of clocks melting down the sides of stuff?"

"Yes, that's the one," replied Doreen with a nod.

"What do you like about his work?" asked Mark.

Doreen replied, "Well, if you spent your entire day in a little office staring at a clock like I do, you'd want to see the darn thing melt off the wall too." She snorted and fixed her glasses.

Mark laughed politely and then continued the increasingly awkward conversation with Doreen for nearly another hour while in another part of the building Tammy was listening from her office.

By the end of that hour, Tammy had her hand over her face

and was shaking her head back and forth while saying, "Mark, you poor, poor, lonely boy. Are you really this desperate for companionship? First Samantha last night and now Doreen. You certainly aren't discriminating, are you? I think it's time that I made my move."

CHAPTER 21

▼

Mark was in his bedroom sitting in front of his computer while Pryb paced back and forth with a half-full Pringles can in his hand. He pointed the can at Mark and said, "Here — help me eat these."

Mark took a handful of chips and asked, "Why do we need to eat all of these now?"

Pryb replied in between chews, "You'll see."

He handed Mark the last few chips and shook the crumbs out on the carpet.

"Hey!" exclaimed Mark.

"Sorry, dude. Wasn't thinking."

Pryb then reached into his pocket and pulled out a knife. He opened it absentmindedly with a practiced flick of his wrist and proceeded to cut a small rectangular hole in the side of the can towards the bottom. Mark watched with interest.

The knife was put away and a USB wifi dongle was produced from another pocket. Pryb inserted the antenna side of the cable into the Pringles can and handed Mark the USB side. "Here, plug this in," he commanded.

"What's this for?" asked Mark while plugging it into his computer.

Pryb pointed out of Mark's window and said, "You see that other hill over there. Doreen lives at the top of it. I've already cracked her wifi password. People say that 802.11g is secure, but it isn't. Anyway, the can is just to boost the range so we can tap into it from here."

Mark was feeling guilty again and said so.

Pryb waved his hand dismissively and said, "We aren't stealing anything. She won't even know about it. No one will know about it. Don't worry. You want to know about the Flicker project, right?"

Mark inhaled and exhaled loudly and said, "Yes, alright."

Pryb gave him a thumbs up and said, "My man." He then set the can on the window sill and sighted down it until it was aimed at the next hill top. He stuffed some of Mark's dirty socks along the sides of it to keep it in place. Mark saw this and frowned.

"OK, hop up," said Pryb while motioning to Mark to get out of the way. Mark got up and Pryb slid into the seat, cracked his knuckles, and said, "OK, let's play."

He clicked the mouse a few times, typed a word on the keyboard, and then pressed enter. "OK, we're in."

"Already?" exclaimed Mark.

"Just to Doreen's wifi. Did you know her password was fuzzybutt?"

Mark laughed and said, "Her cat's name — I should have known."

Pryb shook his head, as if lamenting the stupidity of mankind. "So sad," he despaired.

Mark said, "The cat's real name is Stanley — just like yours. Maybe I can call you Fuzzybutt."

Pryb stopped typing again and turned around in his chair to look at Mark. He said, "Maybe you can go to hell." He turned back around and continued typing for a few seconds. He then suddenly asked, "What was Doreen's last name again? You got me all flustered with that fuzzybutt remark."

"Grossman," replied Mark.

Pryb shook his head and said, "So sad. Poor, poor Doreen Grossman. Never stood a chance in life with a name like that, did you?"

AccelTech's remote login screen was now visible on the computer monitor. Pryb typed in "dgrossman" for the user name and "fuzzybutt" for the password. A welcome message appeared and then the command prompt. Pryb balled his hand into a fist and said, "Yes! Got it in one."

Mark stopped biting his nails and said, "Are you kidding me? Are you freaking kidding me? I spent over an hour learning hundreds of facts about Doreen — the most exciting of which is that she plays bingo after church on Sundays — and we got in on the very first piece of information I collected. What the hell?"

Pryb threw up his hands and said, "That's the way it goes, bro. Better to be safe than sorry. Just be glad we got in."

Pryb then resumed his furious typing. Menus were flashing up on the screen and then disappearing just as quickly. Mark was having a hard time keeping up. Suddenly the printer came to life. Pryb pointed to it and said, "That is Brad's journal entries for the last four months. I downloaded the rest in case we need to go back further. I grabbed everyone else's too, just in case. You start reading that while I figure out if this thing is linked to the security system.

Mark frowned and said, "I understand you downloading the journals, but I don't think we should read them. I mean, Brad basically gave me permission to read his, but I don't want to violate the other's privacy."

Pryb shook his head. "Mark, Mark, Mark. Always the boyscout, aren't you? These aren't their diaries, you know. I mean, they wrote them as notes so that others can read them. I checked the permissions — everyone in the group can read each other's notes. The only thing wrong with reading them is that they are top secret and you don't have clearance, but other than that, no worries."

Mark gave a hollow laugh. "Oh, is that all? Well, OK then. If it's only breaking federal laws we are talking about..."

Pryb dismissed Mark with a wave of his hand while saying, "Shoo. Go. Go read the journal and let Uncle Pryb do his thing."

Mark frowned at him, grabbed the journal from the printer, flopped down on his bed, and began to read.

May 30th: Oh my god, why must I write these pointless entries? No one is reading them, are they? Hey you. Yeah, you. You are a schmucko. Go find something else to do.

June 1st: Nothing happened yesterday so I skipped it. No, I tell a lie, I did take a massive dump and overflowed the toilet. I'm not sure how that helps us to find out how the kernel works, but I'm including it here for completeness. Actually, that does give me an idea. What if we used the old memory overflow trick? It's got to be worth a try, right? Hey schmucko, you reading this? Let's go overflow! Yeah, so anyway, today I went over to Steve's house to see him about something. He wasn't home but I met his wife. There is a lady who is looking for some loving.

June 6th: Steve told me about some new guy today, Mark. He is heading up Plan C, something to do with nutrition. I hope he isn't a health food nut. I don't know what to make of him yet. From his security picture, he looks like a bit of a dork. But none of this is relevant to anything, is it? But if I didn't write about stuff like this, I wouldn't have much to write about since I'm a test pilot without anything to test right now. So bored. The guys with the clean, white coats keep telling me they will have something for me to do very soon. We will see.

June 7th: I'm sure whatever bonehead is reading this already knows what happened today, but I'm supposed to write down my thoughts on stuff so here it goes: Holy crap! Wooooohooooo! I finally got to do some work today. Yesss! We tested the Flicker Camera today. So cool. They sealed me in an airtight glass room and told me to pick up this thingy with wires hanging out of it and slowly sweep it around the room like I was trying to document the contents with a video camera. So I did. And holy crap it worked! So cool. We totally saw into another world. Or, another time maybe. The nerds aren't sure. The camera basically showed what our room used to look like when it was still an abandoned school, so the first assumption is that we are somehow looking at the past. Since the school looks disused, that would put it within a few years from now. OK, this is not quite as cool as seeing the future, I'll grant you, but damn it's still cool. I hope they make this thing portable next. No, wait, I hope they figure out how to send me there. How cool would that be? I'd be just like a terminator. Who am I going to kill first? Hmm. Probably the dork who decided that these logs were worthwhile.

June 8th: The boneheaded janitor over waxed the floor. Several sprains and a few broken bones. I missed the fun since I came in late. I was doing someone else. Something else. I talked to that dude Mark. Tammy was hitting on him, poor guy. Actually, between you and me, I think she's pretty hot. A little thick, but still hot. Certainly better than the rest of the rejects here. Too bad she hates me. And her hair is like a life form all to itself. She can't read this, can she? Hey Tammy, you're hot. Let's hook up!

June 9th: Oh shut up I have a hangover.

June 10th: Really, really bored.

June 13th: Had a really, really nice crap today.

June 14th: OK, listen, I've got nothing to do while the nerds figure out our next move, and there is only so much I can talk about my bowel movements. I'm going to start skipping days now. Deal with it, schmucko.

June 17th: I'm really enjoying my morning workouts. I hope I don't get busted.

June 21st: OK, I've got actual science to report here so pay attention. They made me a mobile camera so I was able to roam around the building with it today. Too cool. They tried to come up with a way of putting me in a sealed plastic sphere while I did so, but in the end they just wrapped me in aluminum foil and followed me around with fire extinguishers. They wouldn't say why. Honestly, I think they are just trying to give the whole thing a sense of occasion, and I can respect that. So anyway, I toured much of the building with the new portable Flicker Camera but it works wirelessly so I was not able to go too far away before the signal faded. I did manage to visit Mark in the Plan C wing and chase him around with the camera telling him that it will probably give him cancer. For some reason he didn't find that funny. He chased me out and told me he was super busy. He's always super busy. He never even eats in the cafeteria, he just grabs something and runs. Kid is going to work himself into an early grave. I hear he works late most nights too. Dude, seriously, you're Plan C. No one cares what you do. Just enjoy yourself. Meh. Anyway, the camera was cool. We compared the footage we took with the pictures that we had all taken when we'd first moved in. They looked identical as far as we could tell. Weird. Looks like we stumbled onto a portal into the past. I can't wait to slip over there and give myself some winning lottery numbers.

July 4th: I jumped out of an airplane naked today with an American flag parachute. It's symbolism, man, you dig? OK, actually I was just drunk. But so was the pilot, so it's all good.

July 12th: I figured out a cheat in WoW that lets me have nearly godlike powers. No one has ever figured it out before. I'm a genius. No, I'm not telling you how, schmucko.

July 21st: Worried about Mark. Dude looks seriously stressed. I know he is married but maybe Tammy should throw him some love. Just a thought.

July 22nd: Had a rare conversation with Mark today. He taught me a new word: strumpet. And there I was thinking I knew everything there was to know about vulgarity. He said the misses is giving him a hard time about working so much. I told him to stuff work, and then stuff his wife. He thanked me for my sterling advice. My pleasure, buddy.

July 29th: The end of another boring week. I also ended my morning workouts. Getting too weird. I was starting to feel guilty, which is the weirdest thing of all.

August 1st: The nerds are getting excited again. They have been trying to break into a different world other than the one we have been peering at thus far. Everything they have tried has failed. Somehow, they find this exciting. They say it tells them more about the fundamental structure of the Flicker World. Personally, I think it just means another boring week for me. I wish Mark would visit more. He is a bit of a prude but at least he doesn't actively avoid me like most of the nerds here. Maybe he was right about the practical jokes. Well, too late now. I think I'll put plastic wrap over the toilet bowls again. That's always good for a laugh.

August 2nd: Work was closed today while the janitor sanitized the building. Somehow things got out of hand with the plastic wrap. Some of it clogged up the toilets, it seems. Stuff was floating down the halls. That's all I'm saying about that.

August 3rd: You ever notice how many of my entries have to do with feces? I should probably show this logbook to a good shrink one day and see what they have to say about it.

August 18th: I practically wrestled Mark to the ground today and forced him to eat with me in the cafeteria. He seemed a little more upbeat than usual today. He said that things were coming together with his project and if all goes well he should be able to do his first funding demo in about a month. Good for him. Maybe he'll chill out a little once all this blows over.

August 19th: Tammy slapped me today for no reason at all. Who would have guessed that she knew what strumpet meant?

August 22nd: I kind of miss my morning exercise. At least it was companionship of a sort. I really need to get a life. Maybe I'll join a pottery class. I bet chicks like that sort of thing.

August 25th: I mentioned my memory overflow idea to one of the white coats today. I mean it's simple, right? If we are objects held in memory, then if we can cause a memory overflow error we might be able to push part of our world into another one because our segmented memory space would overflow into theirs. Simple. Anyway, the white coat actually hugged me, which was awkward because it was a dude. Sadly, this is the most action I've had in a few weeks. He said

this was definitely something to consider
and might just be the path for the next big
thing. I asked him if that's the case, then
why hadn't he done something a couple of
months ago when I wrote it in my journal?
Doesn't anyone read my entries? I showed him
the one I meant. See, it says right here:
"Nothing happened yesterday so I skipped it.
No, I tell a lie, I did take a massive dump
and overflowed the toilet. I'm not sure how
that helps us to find out how the kernel
works, but I'm including it here for
completeness. Actually, that does give me an
idea. What if we used the old memory
overflow trick? It's got to be worth a try,
right? Hey schmucko, you reading this? Let's
go overflow!" He didn't seem impressed. What
a schmuck.

September 5th: Remember, remember, the 5th
of September. Or was it November? I can
never remember.

September 8th: Well here's a thing. This
will frizzle your mind. Well, maybe not you
because no one is really reading these
entries as Mr. Huggy proved to me the other
day. Here it is for posterity anyway... We
tried out the third generation Flicker
Camera today. This one has a theoretically
unlimited range. Oh, and we have sound now
too. Booya! When I turned on the camera in
the lab we all jumped like frightened
children when we saw a young girl on the
screen. It was creepy. Sort of like filming
a ghost. She was looking around as if she
were revisiting old times. She looked rather
peaceful until she saw the whiteboard. She
frowned when she read it and quickly found a
marker. Over top of the words "Sally smells

like fish" she scribbled in black marker "No I don't. Bite me!" Needless to say, this was a revelation, and not just for Sally. We have that very same sign in our world without Sally's addition. This throws a monkey wrench and a full set of screwdrivers into our theory that we were seeing into our past. The white coats are practically frothing at the mouth with excitement. I'm a little bummed that my lottery idea probably won't pan out.

September 17th: Well, this was a shitty day, I don't mind telling you. It started out so well, too. Mark had his demonstration today in front of all sorts of top bigwigs. I'm told he did very well and that his project will be fully funded. Way to go, Mark. But here comes the crappy part. While he had been giving his demonstration, Mark's wife (I think her name was Lisa) was broadsided by a drunk driver who had run a red light. The only good thing you could possibly say about it was that she died instantly. Poor Mark found out just after his demonstration. He threw a wobbly right then and there. Passed out. When he finally came to, he wouldn't stop ranting that he should have stopped her from leaving. In the end, they had to drug him and send him home. I think they are giving him a few weeks off to collect his marbles. Damn. No words.

September 21st: Still no sign of Mark. Dude must be totaled. I can't say I blame him. I'm not sure if I would ever be right after something like that. Rumor has it that they had known each other since they were like ten. That's just all sorts of messed up.

September 26th: All kinds of good news

today. They are sending me on an away mission with the latest Flicker Camera. My goal is to seek out a newspaper and find the current date. I know, right? Real James Bond stuff. Oh, and the other bit of news, they are almost done with the first prototype of a Flicker Suit that will let me actually interact with the other world. To my dismay, they say it won't have a red cape. I mean, come on guys. Get with it.

September 27th: Yesterday's mission was a resounding success. Well, apart from the looks people gave me while I was video taping a newspaper. The camera is still anything but subtle. It's about the size of a broadcast quality video camera. Stupidly heavy, too. Luckily, I was wearing a disguise. I was wearing a fake Fox News name badge. Most people saw it and said, "Oh, it's just Fox News," and left me alone. So back to the newspaper — it was today's! I could only film the cover since I could not touch the version from the other world, but it had the same cover story. Something about a war in the Middle East. Well, that's not rare. Anyway, I went the extra mile and filmed someone's phone. See, cell phones get their time from the network, and the network is synced to an atomic clock. So a cell phone's time should be pretty damn accurate. I compared theirs to mine, and guess what? Their clock was just about three seconds behind mine. How weird is that? So, we are actually looking at the past but not very far at all. Or some sort of alternate something or other. I'm not really sure anymore. I wanted to do more tests but the lady behind the counter was eyeballing me pretty hard so I left with alacrity.

September 30th: Bored. Bored, bored, bored. The white coats won't let me play with the camera anymore until they update their world view. Seriously, that could take a lifetime. Hurry up, nerds! Oh, and the government has bumped up the security requirements for the project to super duper uber top secret or some crap. I'm surprised they haven't put chips in our brains that explode if we talk about it outside of this room. Crap, I shouldn't be giving them these sorts of ideas.

October 3rd: I wonder how Mark is doing? No one has heard from him. I hope he didn't off himself. That sometimes happens, you know. Not just suicide, either. Married couples who have been married for a long time tend to die within a few years of each other. A well known fact. I think the survivor just sort of loses the will to live.

October 4th: I've been doing some thinking. I know, alert the press. I'm hopefully going to get to try out the new Flicker Suit in a few days. I won't lie, I'm defecating rectangular building blocks just thinking about it. Definitely a little nervous. If they really are using my idea of memory overflow, I'm just curious how they intend to get me back. That's a little worrisome. But I'm also worried about something else. Now, supposedly we can only jump to the next world in this great universal task list — the same one we have been peeping into. Fine. Great. But here is the thing. Wouldn't other worlds also be developing the Flicker Project concurrently to us? I see I have your attention. I hope the white coats are reading my entries. I think they are. All of them have been giving me such strange looks every morning. Anyway, presumably my self from the world below us, what we are calling World(-1), is also going to travel to the next world — our world (which, by the way, we are calling World(0) or World Prime). Anyway, I'm not sure how the brass are going to feel about people from another world jumping into our super secure facility. Somehow, I don't think they are going to offer him a warm cup of coffee and send him on his way. Poor bastard. But that is just my speculation. It is clear now from our experiments that AccelTech does not exist in World(+1), so maybe it doesn't exist in World(-1) either. All the same, the day I travel over there is going to be pretty damn interesting, bank on that.

October 12th: Come on, nerds! Slap some duct tape on that suit and let's get going. I'm getting antsy.

October 17th: Mark is back! Dude looks like he's been in a prison camp for a month. He's all malnourished and stuff. Of course that strumpet, Tammy, was trying to pick him up as soon as he returned. I had to chase her away for his own good. It's not at all because I'm a jealous bastard. Nope, nothing of the sort. He was asking me about the Flicker Project. Of course, since we have all gone super top secret, I told him absolutely nothing about the project. My lips are sealed. Anyway, I have to go. I have a date with the owner of the coffee shop I was at the other day for the project. Turns out she was giving me the eyeball for another reason. Now where did I put that Fox News badge?

Mark set down the journal and pinched the bridge of his nose. He blinked a few times while he tried to sort out where and when he was.

Pryb heard him rustling and paused the game that he had been playing to talk to Mark. He swiveled the chair around and said, "I didn't want to disturb you; you looked fully engrossed. Good reading?"

Mark shook his head and blinked heavily. "Interesting. Definitely interesting. It gave me a lot to think about. I think it's sort of good and bad news for me. The other world is not really in our past, it's more of an alternate present as near as I can work out. So I can't travel back in time to stop Lisa's death or even just to spend more time with her. But, there might be an alternate reality Lisa out there for me, which is hopeful." He shrugged.

Pryb thought about this and said, "Yeah, but maybe she died there too, or maybe she didn't but there is an alternate reality Mark who won't be too pleased about sharing his woman, not even with himself."

Mark pinched the bridge of his nose again and said, "I don't know, dude. My head hurts. We'll just take it one step at a time. Did you learn anything about the security system?"

Pryb nodded and said, "Yes, everything." He smirked and expanded on this by saying, "You once told me a hopefully fictitious story about a nuclear power plant with three completely independent fail-safe systems that nevertheless failed because the installer cut a corner and wired them all to the same power circuit since he was falling behind schedule and really did not see the point in wiring them independently anyway. Well, this is very much along those lines. As you've said, there is both a fingerprint scanner and retinal scanner, an ID card reader, and a password requirement. It would be extremely difficult for us to acquire or fake all that identification. Fortunately for us, we can bypass all of them with just one thing."

"What's that?" asked Mark, obediently.

Pryb smirked again and said, "Fuzzybutt."

Mark stared at him.

Pryb gestured to the computer and explained, "The security system is controlled by the central server, and we are in the server right now. I can re-write what I want, turn off what I want, delete what I want."

Mark stared for another long second and then blinked. "So, that's it? We're in?"

"Yep."

"Well, that was easy. So, what's the plan, then?"

"We'll have to talk about that, but as far as the security system goes, I'll give you the admin code for the scanners so you can register yourself as a valid user at your convenience. Then it's simply a matter of creating a card, a password, and tying them both to the user code that was created by the scanner. Easy."

"How did you learn all of this stuff?" asked Mark, impressed.

"Simple, I just typed 'man' — that's short for manual by the way — followed by the thing that I was interested in. Sometimes you can just type 'help'. People are stupid. Programmers have to make it easy for us." He grinned again.

"It's nice to see you enjoying yourself, Pryb. But all kidding aside, I don't know how to thank you enough for the help."

"Well, you know what they say, a good friend will help you move, but a true friend will help you move a body."

"Oh god, I hope it won't come to that," fretted Mark as he bit his nail absentmindedly.

"No worries," said Pryb soothingly, "What could possibly go wrong?"

Mark bit his fingertip and drew blood.

CHAPTER 22

---- ▼ ----

Anything would have been better, Brad thought to himself as he put on the Flicker Suit for the first time. It could have been sleek. It could have been silver with burgundy accents. It could even have had a cape. Instead, he was being forced to wear this goofy looking thing, with its bulky white body and round white helmet. He looked in the mirror and the Stay Puft Marshmallow Man stared back at him. He sighed and entered the main room of the laboratory.

He was flanked by Steve as soon as he walked through the door. He could tell that Steve was suppressing a laugh. Brad said to him, "Seriously, boss, this thing is awful. I feel like it should say 'NO FRILLS' across my back. This is seriously going to ruin my image, you realize that, don't you?"

Steve smirked and said, "No, no. It suits you. You look like a regular Don Juan."

"Yeah. Don Juan's dead and bloated carcass is more like it. Who designed this thing, anyway?"

Steve said that he did not know, and then turned slightly and secretly gave a thumbs-up to his nephew, Laslo. Laslo in turn looked pleased as punch at the sight of his creativity come to life.

Brad looked around the room but saw no sign of Mark. Well, of course he would not be here, he thought — he was not part of this group after all. Still, he did wish that Mark could have come; he could have really used an ally.

Deflated in spirit but inflated in appearance, Brad stepped up to the center of a two-foot high podium. There had been some debate as to whether or not to use the bullet proof capsule again, but in the end the security squad had won the argument on the basis that the capsule would make it difficult to shoot anything that might come across from another Flicker World. The test pilot had argued that it would also make it that much easier for something to shoot them, or for that matter, for them to accidentally shoot him. His objections were noted and dismissed, as was military custom when confronted with common sense.

Brad scanned the room again. There was roughly an equal number of white coats and green shirts. The white coats were armed with their trusty tablets, and the green shirts with their trusty M16s. Brad really hoped that the padding in his suit could stop a bullet.

He cursed himself for letting real scientific observations slip into his daily log. After all, he was the genius that had first brought up the notion that there could be people from World(-1) that were about to try the same experiment, likely at the very same time. The military latched onto this intel and mutated the logic by also surmising that the people of World(-1) could be anything, maybe not even human. Perhaps they could be human but with the goal of dominating our world and stripping it of resources to bring back to their own world. Brad knew that this just happened to be one of the stated potential uses for the Flicker Project, but since we were the good guys then it was OK, unlike those thieving bastards from World(-1).

Brad sighed one last time, lifted his left arm, and pushed a button on his sleeve. He then spoke clearly for all to hear, his voice being broadcast over the room's intercom system, "Ready to begin trial one of Flicker Suit Mark One. Trial to begin in five, four, three, two, one. Pushing the big, red button now."

He pushed a big, red button on his sleeve. Instantly, he turned semi transparent, much like a ghost. He tried to ignore all the rifles that were pointed in his direction as he looked around the room.

Three seconds later, he turned mostly solid again except around the edges. It was almost as if God had tried to put two of him almost but not quite in the same space at the same time.

Suddenly Brad separated into two semitransparent Brads. One of which turned around and started walking to the back of the room, while another one was left standing there, frozen in horror at the sight of so many guns pointed at him.

Everyone in the room heard a faint, "Oh hell no!" just before one Brad slapped at the big, red button on his sleeve and disappeared. The remaining Brad continued to explore the room, although he could still sense the guns pointed at him behind his back.

He walked over to the now famous white board and gently touched it. He felt the pressure on his finger tips from the board, but when he pushed harder his hand pushed right through it, which freaked him out immensely. He pulled his hand back quickly. Both it and the board were unharmed.

He then gently began to rub out the words with his gloved hand. It took him two full minutes to do this, all the while he was trying to ignore the voice in his helmet that kept insisting that he stop messing around and continue with the experiment.

The next part was the tricky one. After many tries, he was able to grasp a black marker with just enough force to hold it firmly but not so hard that it pushed through his hand and dropped onto the floor.

Carefully, he wrote the following: "Sally I'm sorry. The truth is I still love you. Can you forgive me?"

The voice in his head was now screaming something about irreversibly altering the course of history, but he continued to ignore it and began the experiment in earnest. He had already touched the board and manipulated an object, so those were off the list. He was supposed to close and lock the door, but he conveniently forgot about that one — after all, how would Sally get back in?

He moved on to the next item, which was to turn one desk upside down and stack it on top of another. This proved very hard to do. The desk weighed too much so his hands kept pushing straight through it. However, he eventually did succeed by using both of his forearms to lift it, which had apparently provided enough surface area to prevent the desk from pushing through. Unfortunately, as he was flipping the desk over it bumped his big, red button and shot him back to his own world, World(0).

This could have been a deadly error had he rematerialized in the middle of something else. Fortunately the white coats had thought ahead and had cleared out the test area ahead of time. Just the same, they later installed a safety cover over the button as another precaution.

Brad instinctively squatted down in a defensive crouch and looked around. Damn, he was back in the real world again. He saw the green shirts rushing toward him and instantly raised his hands above his head. One of them edged a little closer and read the words that had been scrawled on his chest in marker just before the experiment. They read "I am a big aardvark."

"It's OK," one shouted, "He's ours." The men relaxed and lowered their guns.

The writing had been Steve's idea, of course. He had picked a person at random from the crowd. They had picked another, and that person picked another until they had five. Each of them wrote one word on him. Steve had started with "I", knowing that something entertaining was likely to follow. He had really been grinning when the next three people followed his lead with "am a big". Unfortunately, the last person had been Roller Girl, whose sense of humor was as bad as her balance. She had written "aardvark" and had laughed so hard afterward that she had fallen, leaving a black line trailing down from the "k" all the way down one of Brad's legs. This, at the very least, had made the password even more unique.

Steve came quickly up to Brad and shook his hand. He said loudly for all to hear, "Excellent job, Brad. Things might not have gone exactly to plan, but I call that a successful first attempt. Well done." He then leaned closer to Brad, who by now had removed his helmet, and whispered into his ear, "I know you could hear me shouting at you, you bastard, because that bulbous helmet of yours would wobble slightly every time I did. Next time, stick with the plan, OK?"

Brad merely grinned in return.

CHAPTER 23

———————▼———————

Tomorrow just might be the big day, thought Mark as he finished reading Brad's notes. He set them on the bed beside him and scratched his chin with the backside of his fingers.

Pryb heard the rustling of paper behind him and swiveled his chair to face Mark. He asked with a grin, "So, what did that crazy guy have to say today?"

Mark picked up the notes, cleared his throat, and began to read the pertinent passages.

```
I completed the third successful test of the
Flicker Suit today. The white coats are keen
to work out the timing issues so they can
fully send me to World(+1). Right now I'm
still a big, blobby ghost in both worlds
whenever I activate the suit. The nerds say
that this is because I'm flicking back and
forth between both worlds, so I'm only
halfway in each world at any given moment.
All I know is, it is the creepiest thing
ever. Seriously very gross.

While the white coats consider this to be
only a partial success, the green shirts are
unsurprisingly fascinated by this effect,
mainly because it means that I can now walk
through walls. To that end, they are slowing
down our progress in perfecting the suit in
order to explore this effect at length.
Lucky me.
```

They asked me what it feels like to walk through walls, and for once in my life, words had failed me. The best I could come up with was "gross" and "dreadful" preceded by several expletives. Now that I'm less agitated, maybe I'll try to explain it more clearly for the sake of posterity.

Actually, before I do that, maybe I should add some context. Normally, a person can't walk through walls since two objects cannot occupy the same space. Simple enough, right? But when you consider that matter is mostly empty space, it makes you wonder why this is so.

According to basic atomic principles, atoms have a positively charged nucleus that is orbited by one or more negatively charged electrons. Relative to the size of the nucleus, the electrons are stupidly far away. For a very rough idea, consider a pea in the middle of a racetrack, or a basketball in the center of Manhattan.

As everyone knows, these electrons whiz around the nucleus and form the outer extents of the atom. This outer shell is negatively charged because of the electrons' charge.

Consider your hand and a table, which are both made up of atoms, of course. If there is so much space between the electrons and the nucleus of these atoms, why can't you put your hand through the table? Wouldn't the parts of the atom just sort of flow around each other? If you bang your fist on the table right now then you will see the answer is no.

Wow, look at me, I feel like a professor and stuff. I would have been a great elementary science teacher, don't you think? I'd have little kids karate chopping the hell out of their desks right now. How fun would that be?

Well, anyway, it's not to be. But going back to atoms... the thing is, the electrons are creating a wall of negativity as they whiz around. Since like charges repel, when the atoms of your hand and the atoms of the desk come in proximity, they repel each other due to the electric force. Think of the electrons as a very strong force field around the nucleus. When objects touch, these force fields are pushing back against one another.

Which brings us to me and my magical marshmallow suit. The white coats think that since atoms also sort of vibrate around randomly even in solid objects, it means that the placement of the atoms in World(0) (our world) and the placement of atoms in World(+1) are sure to be different. (This random motion, by the way, is called temperature. No, really it is. Go look it up some time. It's crazy stuff.) Anyway, any idiot can see that the placement of the atoms are different because even at a macroscopic level the room looks completely different in World(+1) than it does in ours. However, the nerds assure me that this weird side effect would still work even if the rooms had looked identical.

So, the deal is, since I'm time sharing between worlds, I can push a small way into an object in one world, then when I flip I can push a little more since some of the atoms that were in my way are bound to be in a slightly different position. If there is only air in one world, then it makes it even easier. A wooden wall in both worlds takes a lot of effort and feels like walking through very thick oatmeal while simultaneously drinking oatmeal, breathing oatmeal, and having oatmeal pooling around my heart, causing it to almost stop. It is seriously, seriously disturbing. I hate it.

I think the worst part about it is that when it is happening, it feels so bad that it makes me want to rush through it, but the faster I move, the worse things become. It's the difference between swimming under water and belly flopping onto the surface of it.

I have also tried the suit with steel in one world and air in the other. That feels the same as a wooden wall in both worlds but substitute chilled mercury for oatmeal. I have refused to try it with steel in both places. I did try it with my hand, though. I have a nice scar to show for it.

Naturally, being the suspicious bastards that they are, the green shirts have made us install cameras and motion sensors in the lab to alert us if my World(-1) counterpart decides to pop in for a visit again. Unlike before, we can't count on him arriving at the same time as my experiments. Likely they have switched to a randomized schedule to avoid this, as that is exactly what we would do.

Well class, the lesson is over for today. For homework I want each of you to write a five page essay on why your teacher is so awesome and why you all want to be like him when you grow up. Class dismissed.

Mark finished reading and said, "Well, what are your thoughts? I'm kind of thinking that if I can get in there, all I have to do is turn it on and stroll on out through the wall. I'm not sure about the cameras and motion detectors, though. Sounds bad."

Pryb said, "I think I'd like to meet that test pilot one day and have a beer with him, that's what I think. As for the newly added security..." Pryb held up a finger "...give me a moment." He spun around in the chair and typed furiously on the computer keyboard for a little over three minutes and then swiveled back around.

"OK, all sorted out."

"What is?" asked Mark.

Pryb tilted his head. "The motion sensors and cameras. They're on the main system too, the idiots. I programmed the sensors to turn off when you swipe to enter the room, and turn back on when you leave. The cameras will freeze the last image they see when you swipe to enter the room, but continue to superimpose a current timestamp. They will unfreeze when you leave. Simple. I've done this before a dozen times. It's the same system they use at the embassy in... well, that's not really important. The important thing is that this works in our favor. They are relying on tech for security, which means that once you are in that room, you shouldn't have to worry about the guards strolling in and noticing their priceless prototype has walked out the door... or through it in this case."

Mark narrowed his eyes and asked seriously, "What is it again that you actually do for a living, Pryb?"

Pryb looked offended. "You know that. I work for Home Emporium installing cabinets, counter tops, and flooring."

"Yeah... right..." replied Mark without emotion as he studied his friend's face. "Well, we'll leave it at that, then."

Pryb nodded. "Yes, I think that's for the best. Anyway, I'm going to split and let you get your rest. Tomorrow is a big day for you, right? I take it you're ready to act?"

"Yep, you know me," answered Mark. "Strike while the iron's hot."

"Cool. I'll work out the details while you're at work. Later, bro."

"Later."

CHAPTER 24

―――――――▼―――――――

"What are you doing here at this time of night?" asked Tammy after walking into the cafeteria and spotting Mark huddled in the back near the vending machines. She was peering at him with one eye though the tangle of hair that was partially obscuring her face.

Mark jumped a little and said rapidly, "What? Oh, hey Tammy. Fancy meeting you here. It's like fate or something, right? Ha-ha-ha." He scratched the back of his head and grinned nervously. Tammy's visible eye squinted with the appearance of suspicion.

Tammy took a long second to think of how to play this, and then smiled warmly at Mark as she took a seat opposite him. "Yes, definitely fate," she agreed. "Who would have thought the cafeteria would become our special place together?"

Mark gave another nervous laugh and said, "Who indeed?"

Tammy took one of his potato chips and chewed it while gazing thoughtfully at him, which obviously made him even more nervous. You're doing something really naughty tonight, aren't you my little Mark, thought Tammy as she swallowed the potato chip.

"You still haven't answered my question, though," she stated coldly as she leaned over the table toward Mark.

Mark leaned back slightly and asked, "Question? What question was that?"

"What are you doing here so late tonight?"

"Me? Oh, just working late. Stuff to do, not enough hours in the day. You know how it is. How about you?"

"Same. Doing some stuff."

Mark smiled and nodded. He got up from the table and said hastily, "Well, since we both have stuff to do, I guess we should go do it, eh?" He started to walk past Tammy on the way toward the door when Tammy suddenly stood up beside him and stopped him.

She tossed her hair to one side and said, "I'll be frank with you, Mark. I realize that Brad makes me out to be some kind of floozy, but it isn't like that. I have never slept with anyone here. All I'm looking for is a little companionship. That's all. I'm sure you know how it is, right? When you're smart, it's hard to find someone that understands you."

Mark avoided her eyes and said, "Well, actually, I guess I was lucky like that. I had Lisa all this time. But now that she's gone, I think I understand what you mean. Look, I'll be frank in return, I don't have anything against you and I'm definitely interested in getting to know you, but right now really isn't a good time. My mind is still a mess, you understand."

Tammy forced a smile and moved out of Mark's way. "Of course. I understand. But if fate brings us together again in this cafeteria, I hope we can talk again soon."

Mark smiled. "Of course. Well, I've got to go back to work. See you around."

"See you," replied Tammy with a lazy wave. "Good luck with your stuff."

Mark answered back as he walked away, "Yep, good luck with yours too."

Mark left the cafeteria and walked briskly back to his own lab. He took a few steps inside and a voice called out to him, "Mark, what are you doing here this late?"

Mark threw up his hands and said, "Jesus Christ, what now?"

Shocked, the voice said remorsefully, "I'm so sorry, Mr. Scottsdale. Am I interrupting you? I am, aren't I? Shall I leave?"

The owner of the voice, Samantha, was hugging her tablet and shrinking back from Mark. Mark saw this and lowered his head in shame. He said apologetically, "No, sorry, I didn't mean to snap at you. I just didn't expect anyone else to be here, is all. Truthfully, I was hoping for a little quiet time to think."

Samantha relaxed slightly and replied, "No, no need to apologize. I understand. I like to stay here after hours as well." She looked around the place for a moment and added, "It's weird, isn't it? How different a place becomes after hours. It takes on a completely different atmosphere. A different soul. More peaceful, but at the same time haunted." She shook her head as if she had said too much and then said, "Well, I'll let you have your peace, sir. From now on, I'll message you if I'm going to be here after hours so we don't disturb one another. Would that be acceptable?"

Mark was still thinking about her eerie but somehow accurate description of the lab and replied a little distractedly, "What? Oh yes. Yes, that would be fine. Sorry again. Thanks for letting me have the room today."

"No problem at all, sir. Any time. See you tomorrow."

"OK, see you tomorrow."

Samantha left. Mark let out a big, long sigh as he sat down in a chair and allowed himself to slide halfway out of it. He sat like that for a few seconds while he collected his thoughts and then pulled himself back upright. OK, he thought, I guess I might as well get this over with. No real reason to wait.

He opened the door to his lab again and peered out into the hallway. He had half expected the voice of Doreen to call out to him asking him why he was there so late, but thankfully it did not. The hallway looked empty. He reminded himself about what Pryb had told him. The best thing he could do would be to act like he belonged there. Act like you own the place, he had said. If you do, people will tend to fall for the spell. You have to believe it, though, deep down in your heart. If you believe, they will believe. Usually.

Mark tried not to sweat when he thought about that "usually." It all sounded very Peter Pan to him. If you believe you can fly, you can. But don't doubt that you can even for a second or the fall is going to hurt.

As he walked down the hallway and around the corner to the entrance to Plan A, he quietly repeated to himself, "I do believe in fairies. I do. I do."

On the other side of the building, Tammy shook her head and then repositioned her headphones slightly. "Fairies?" she asked herself in puzzlement.

Mark walked up to the main door of Plan A and swiped his card without hesitation. He did not look around before doing this. Pryb had drilled that much into his head. Don't look around like you are checking to see if anyone is watching. If they are and they see you looking shifty then you are toast. However, if a guard sees you swiping a badge and entering a room, well, that's just business as usual, isn't it? I mean, obviously you are allowed to go in there because the door let you in. Remember, act like you own the place.

So, without glancing around, Mark entered the code and let his eyes and fingerprints be scanned. The green light lit up and the door unlocked. Mark walked through and gently closed the door behind him. He then put his back against the door and slid down it, landing heavily on his butt.

He shook his head and said softly, "I'm an idiot. What the heck am I doing?"

Across the building, Tammy heard this and was wondering the same thing.

Mark then reminded himself why he was there. He thought back to the insufferable pain he had felt after losing Lisa. He glanced over in the direction of the prototype Flicker Suit and his resolve stiffened. He stood up and dusted himself off. He then rubbed his palms together several times and said, "Right, let's go."

Tammy, who could only hear what was going on, was wondering what he was about to do. She checked another screen which showed his triangulated position as being somewhere inside of Plan A's lab. "What are you doing, you naughty boy?" she said to her dark, empty office.

Mark started to walk toward the suit and then remembered himself and detoured to the nearby superfluous light panel. He used an electric screwdriver to remove the bolts from one of the bottom panels and gently moved it aside. As Pryb had expected, there was room behind the panel about the thickness of the wall. This would be a good hiding place in case there is some sort of alarm on the suit.

Pryb had said that most people expect the bad guy to be well away from the loud alarms by the time they get there, so hiding out inside the room was the best way to go. Mark wondered again at what his friend got up to during his frequent vacations.

Mark replaced the panel but left the screws and the screwdriver in a nearby drawer. He then walked over to the suit and stood in front of it for a full minute while he mustered up his bravery.

He glanced at his watch. Damn, he was fifteen minutes behind schedule. Pryb was going to lecture him about that, he just knew it.

He cringed slightly as he gently lifted up the suit. There was no alarm. That was a slight relief, but Pryb had warned him that there could be a silent alarm, so it was most important that he hurried as soon as he touched the suit. Knowing this, Mark quickly put on the suit and the helmet.

In her office, Tammy cursed as "Loss of signal" flashed on one of the screens in front of her.

Mark lifted his left arm and quickly familiarized himself with the controls. Power was at 100%. Emergency oxygen was at 100%. It seemed ready to go. He flipped up the protective cover and put his finger on the big, red button. He thought about Lisa and pushed it.

The world went strange. He staggered backward but managed to catch his balance. He was seeing double vision, but not the type you get after drinking too much. He was seeing both the lab and the classroom at the same time.

As much as he wanted to explore a little and get used to this, he was still worried about the possibility of there being a silent alarm and some very angry people with guns arriving at any moment, so he quickly found the back wall to the room and put his hand up to it. He put some pressure on it and watched in horror as his hand slowly merged with the wall. He reminded himself to stay calm and move slowly. If he wanted to survive this, he knew he had to do at least that much.

He calmly pulled his hand back and inspected it. He could not see his hand through the glove of the suit, but it felt fine. He shrugged, although an outside observer would not have noticed this because of all the padding in the suit.

Brad was right, thought Mark, this really is an awful suit. It was like someone had stuffed a space suit full of cotton until it bulged in all the wrong places.

Well, time to go, he thought. With much effort of will, he forced himself into the wall, arms first. He was pushing through the same cinder block wall in both worlds, so it was not an easy thing to do.

Brad had said that the experience of wood was like oatmeal. To Mark, walking through cinder block felt like being buried in wet concrete. He started to panic as his torso merged with the wall. He was instinctively holding his breath.

He could feel the block flowing around and through his organs. It's a terrible thing to be aware of one's own organs. He could feel the grittiness of the block wall around his heart, which felt like it was struggling to continue to pump.

Mark was now seriously panicked. He tried to take a quick breath and couldn't. His heart stopped. He leaned forward to take another step but his leg didn't want to move. He blacked out.

Slowly, very slowly, the leaning of his body continued to pull him through the wall. As more and more of him emerged from it, his progress sped up until he was fully outside of the building. He spun gently as he fell to the ground and landed heavily on his back. He was unharmed by the fall thanks to the padding of the suit. Unfortunately, the suit then began to electrocute him.

Pryb, who had been lurking in the shadows, came running over to aid his friend. He checked his watch. There would be a good ten minutes until the next patrol came around. Good.

He saw his friend spasm for a few seconds and then was still. No, the spasming came back a second time. And a third. Pryb grabbed the suit by the shoulders and hissed, "Dude. Come out of it. Are you alright? Speak to me. Don't you die, you bastard." He shook him some more.

Mark opened his eyes. He was being shaken violently. Had they found him? They must have. Yes, they had just tasered him, he was sure of that.

"Come on, buddy. Speak to me."

"Pryb?" questioned Mark, once he could get a good look at his attacker.

Because of the dark, and because Mark was only 50% in his world, Pryb could not see clearly into the visor of the suit, nor could he hear Mark through the visor. He grabbed the upper arms of the suit more firmly in order to get a really good shake and felt his fingers ooze into the suit. He let go and jumped back.

Mark called out, "It's cool, dude. I'm fine."

Nothing.

"Hello?"

Nothing.

"Damn. I'm an idiot." He pushed a button on his left sleeve and said, "Can you hear me now?"

Pryb looked around in panic. "Shhh! Yes I can hear you. Now keep it down," he hissed.

Mark turned a knob on his sleeve. "Is this OK?"

Pryb nodded while scanning the surroundings. "Yes, fine. You OK? Good. Let's get out of here like now. We'll talk in the car."

Pryb then quickly wrapped a black poncho around Mark and they both walked nonchalantly over to Mark's car. Just to be safe, Mark crouched down in the back seat while Pryb drove them out of the lot.

Mark secretly thanked his boss, Steve, while he and Pryb escaped unhindered. This is because it had been Steve's idea to forgo outside gates and guards. His reasoning had been that fences and guards outside the building would only draw unwanted attention to the place and make the wrong sort of people curious about what might be inside.

Mark checked the suit's battery meter and saw that it was at 87%. He pushed the big, red button in order to return fully to World(0) and to conserve power.

Now sitting up, he said, "Dude, the hard part turned out to be the easy part and the easy part turned out to be the hard part. I just walked in there and took the suit, no problem at all. However, walking through the wall nearly killed me. Actually, I think it did kill me. I'm pretty sure of that. I think the suit zapped me and got my heart going again. All I know is, that was, by far, the worst thing I've ever done. Ever. By a long way."

"Yeah, well, you were dying to see Lisa again, anyway," said his supposedly best friend, flippantly.

"Dude," said Mark.

Pryb glanced back at Mark for a second and then said, "Sorry. Didn't know what else to say to that. 'Glad you didn't die' just sounds so lame."

"It's alright. Anyway, what's the plan now?"

"You got any kind of computer system in that suit? Like something to access the Internet?"

"No. I'm pretty sure I don't."

"Damn. Plan B it is, then."

"Oh great. As long as it doesn't have to do with bugs."

"Bugs?"

"Oh nothing, just an inside joke. So what's plan B?"

Pryb pulled over and stopped the car in front of a business. He pointed to it.

Mark looked at it and said, "No. No, no, no. Not dressed like this."

Pryb replied tersely. "You almost died to see Lisa already. Are you really going to let a little embarrassment stop you now?"

Mark dropped his huge, white, bulbous head and said, "No, I guess not. Let me see if it exists on the other side." He pushed the big, red button and expected the same double image as before, but everything was fairly clear. He checked his gauges. The suit was definitely active. He asked Pryb, who replied, "Yep, you are definitely in ghost mode, although maybe it's the light but you look slightly more solid than you did at the lab."

Mark ignored this and read the sign aloud, "Watt's Up Internet Cafe. Yep, looks like it exists in the other world too." He sighed and said, "OK, I'll be right back."

Mark got out of the car, closed the door, took three steps, smacked his visor with his hand, walked back to the car, opened the door, and said, "Can I borrow twenty bucks?"

With money now in hand, Mark tried to think of what he was going to say as he walked to the entrance of the cafe. About a foot from the door, another thought struck him and he quickly walked back to the car and got back inside. "Dude, the money is in your world. I need it in World(+1)."

Pryb frowned. "Sorry, I missed that. I'm not used to thinking in multiple dimensions. Actually, now that you mention it, there are going to be two attendants that see you at the same time, aren't there? That could get weird."

"No doubt," replied Mark.

"OK, let's think this through," began Pryb. "We will take one problem at a time. I can distract the attendant in this world, so you won't have to worry about the one here. OK, that's easy. But how do you pay?"

"I don't."

Pryb pointed at Mark and said, "Now you're speaking my language. Ah, I know what you're thinking. You're thinking you can flip over to this world completely and sneak in while I'm distracting the attendant. Once inside the privacy of a booth, you can flip over and do your search. That could work."

Mark nodded and said, "Yes, that could work, I think. But how do I get back out?"

Pryb shrugged. "I'm sure you'll think of something."

"Great," said Mark sarcastically. "Sounds like a plan."

Mark flipped over to being fully in World(0). Pryb told him to wait until he saw the attendant running out of the cafe, then he was to run (as best as he could) into the Internet cafe undetected. This was starting to sound like a bad idea to Mark.

Pryb got out of the car and opened his trunk. After a few moments he closed the trunk and walked over to a store just to the left of the cafe. With a smile, he lit a Molotov cocktail and threw it down in front of the store. It landed mostly on the sidewalk.

A moment later the cafe attendant saw a frantic man run into his cafe while shouting, "fire!"

The attendant looked around in a panic. Unfortunately, he had no water readily available and his only fire extinguisher had been used only two days ago to put out an electrical fire in the networking closet. As if reading his thoughts, the frantic man said, "Forget about water. The fire is still small. Just help me stamp it out, will you? Hurry!"

Now feeling the panic, the attendant followed the frantic man out of the cafe and helped him to stamp out the fire. Meanwhile, behind his back, a giant marshmallow ran into the cafe and hid inside one of the booths.

After resting for a moment, Mark unplugged the computer so that he would not be distracted by two screens showing different information once he activated the suit.

Then, pausing only to take a deep breath, Mark pushed the big, red button. The world shimmered but largely looked the same. The computer screen was on again, although it looked to be about half as bright as it should have been.

Mark began his search. First he checked the obituaries on the day of Lisa's death. He checked twice, in fact, and could find no mention of her. He was so relieved by this that he started to cry inside of his helmet, which then caused the visor to fog up. To fix this, he turned on the suit's cooling function momentarily to clear the visor.

With a little more searching he found her name and picture on a few social networking sites, but the information was sparse. The Lisa he had known had been very private, and it seemed that this one was the same. In fact, her home town had been listed as Mars on one of the sites. He smiled at that, and then frowned. Oh well, at least he now knew that she existed in this world. That was good news.

It took some time, but he was eventually able to piece together her address from information scattered over the Internet, mostly by her friends and family. Mark was good at computers, but this search would have taken him much longer had Pryb not given him some suggestions on the best approach to take. Mark was really starting to respect and fear his friend. It was like waking up one day and discovering that your best friend was a super villain. Exactly like that, in fact.

His mission now accomplished, Mark committed the address to memory and then erased his search history. Now it was time to turn his mind toward making an exit. He had no way to contact Pryb, which was a pity. The fire gambit was unlikely to work twice in any case. He thought briefly of walking through the wall, but the idea of doing so revolted him. He would not be doing that again unless he had absolutely no choice. If only he could fully flip between worlds, he thought.

Mark decided he needed more information before he could act, so he stealthily peeked out of the booth to gain some intelligence. The cafe seemed empty in both worlds except for the attendants. He had not heard anyone else enter since he had been in the cafe, so he could only assume that it was empty. That was good.

He looked to his left and saw the back door, which was for emergency use only and was alarmed. Damn. There was also a fuse box in the hallway. Now there was a thing. He went back into the room to think.

The obvious thing to do was to shut off the lights at the breaker and try to sneak past the attendant in the dark. If he did such a thing with the suit active then he would make half the sound and would be even less visible in the dark. That would definitely be a plus. Of course, that would also mean dodging two attendants at once. Well, it was probably worth the risk.

With this ludicrous plan now made, Mark crept out of the booth and flipped the breaker. Since his suit was already active, he had to swat at the switch quickly in order to get it to flip without his finger passing through it, but when it did finally flip, it tripped the breaker in both worlds. He heard a muffled, "What the hell?" from the attendants in near synchronicity. Hmm, probably the same guy in both worlds, then. Interesting.

Mark walked as quietly and quickly as he could down the hallway. He needed to clear the hallway before the attendant entered it or they would end up passing right next to each other. That is assuming that the attendant would first make his way to the breaker, which was reasonable.

Mark made it ninety percent of the way down the hall when a rectangle of light was suddenly pointed directly at him from a few feet away. The attendant was using his phone as a flashlight and was undoubtedly seeing Mark.

There was nothing for it now, thought Mark. He raised his hands menacingly and moaned loudly while whisking passed the attendant, who swore in response and dropped his phone.

Mark ran to the door. It was locked. He cursed the competency of the attendant and eased his way through it. Weirdly enough, it felt like water.

He took one step outside and an unseen person immediately tried to grab his hand and pull him into an alleyway, but the hand squished right through it instead.

"Oh god, that's disgusting. Don't just stand there, marshmallow head, follow me," said a voice with some disgust and much anxiety.

Pryb led Mark through a maze of alleys and fences until they emerged a few blocks away. They found Mark's car and quickly jumped inside.

Mark turned off the suit. The battery was almost dead. He took the helmet off and panted. After a while, he said, "I think that went well, what do you think?"

Pryb just gave him a look, put the car into gear, and quietly drove off into the night.

After a moment Pryb asked, "So, you got the address?"

"Yep, I got it. She's maybe twenty minutes away."

Pryb glanced at the clock on the car's radio and said, "We probably have time. You want to go there now?"

Mark checked the battery gauge again and said, "It's no use tonight. The battery on this thing is almost dead. I'll need what's left to get back inside. I can't say I'm looking forward to that."

"Why don't you just keep the thing?" suggested Pryb.

Mark blinked. "You're asking me why I don't just keep a top secret military prototype? Is that what you're asking me?"

"Yes."

"Well, for starters, someone is bound to notice it missing. And you know who gets looked at first when that happens? The employees — especially the new guy. That's me, by the way."

"Good point," admitted Pryb.

"Besides," added Mark, "I don't think I have a charge cord that will work with this thing."

"It's not just USB then?" asked Pryb with a smirk.

"No," answered Mark. "That's the military for you. They like to go the proprietary route at ten times the expense."

"Makes you proud to be an American, don't it?" chimed Pryb.

Mark merely grinned in reply and collapsed into the back seat from exhaustion.

They arrived back at AccelTech some time later after an uneventful drive. Mark had fallen asleep in the back seat. Pryb woke him up by knocking on his helmet.

Mark sighed and said, "I don't want to go through the wall

again. I really don't."

Pryb shrugged. "I don't blame you, bro, but what else can you do?" He thought for a moment and added, "Although, I suppose we could go back to your house, switch off the cameras, come back here, sneak past the guards, and... No, that won't work. The security system is designed to alarm if the same person tries to enter a room twice without first leaving. I learned that the hard way. See here..."

Pryb pointed at a scar on his forearm in the shape of a dog's bite.

Mark shook his head. "Forget it. It doesn't matter. I'm beat. Let me just get this over with. If I don't see you in a half hour or so... well, use your own judgment."

"Just look for a softer spot in the wall. I'll wait."

Mark shook his head while getting out of the car and said, "Just look for the softer spot in the masonry wall, he says."

Mark mumbled curses to himself the entire walk to the building. Everything seemed quiet. Pryb had told him where to walk as to not be seen by the external cameras. Pryb would delete any records of them at a later time, but there was always a chance that a keen guard could be monitoring them live. As it stood, the approach of a car at this time of night could have already raised some suspicions.

Mark was already in dimensional shift mode. He surveyed the walls in both worlds and then smacked his helmet with his hand again. The version of the building in World(+1) had windows. He had not seen them from the inside, probably because they were transparent and the frames were toward the outside of the wall.

He already knew that glass was somehow easy to go through, so hopefully he would not die again if he walked through that part of the wall. Of course, it was still solid block in World(0), so this was not going to be pain free.

Putting his left foot up first, Mark carefully stepped over the window ledge and through the window/wall conglomerate. Strangely, the materials were dissimilar enough that the experience was not completely horrible — only mostly horrible. To Mark, it felt like he was merging with sandy pudding. As he did so, he thought, "This can not be good for the human body."

Mark was nearly through the wall when the battery to the suit went dead and he was captured inside the wall by the tip of his middle finger. Since he had already been moving away from the wall at speed in the knowledge of a job well done, it came as a surprise to him when his finger tip was suddenly and violently ripped off.

The scream that followed was loud and heartfelt. The blood that appeared was also surprisingly plentiful, as was Mark's panic.

Mark felt adrenaline, endorphins, and probably many other emergency chemicals kick into action. He suddenly moved with razor sharp clarity. He quickly took off his glove and used it to stem the bleeding. He then made his way quickly to the lab's medical unit and haphazardly bandaged his finger. After that, he sprinted over to the wall with an alcohol-soaked napkin and cleaned up the fresh blood. Part of his finger was merged with the wall in one spot. Nothing he could do about that at the moment.

He quickly removed the suit and replaced it on its holding stand. He scanned the area and found a storage bin full of spare gloves. He replaced both of the gloves on the suit and stuffed the old ones into his pocket along with the bloody napkins. Then he ran like an elderly cheetah over to the superfluous light panel and hid himself while trying to bring his breathing back under control.

Minutes passed. No guards came. More time passed. Still nothing. Could they really not have heard that scream, he wondered. He waited a full ten minutes and then finally came out of hiding. This was too stressful by half, he thought as he replaced the screws in the panel and took one last look around to make sure everything was as it should be.

Oh wait! My fingertip! He had almost forgotten. He took the screwdriver over to the wall and began to gently chisel out the offending spot while wearing a grimace of disgust on his face.

He collected the sandy, meaty chunks in another napkin and with some hesitation put it into his pocket with the other refuse.

Now thoroughly spent, Mark took one last look around and then left the room. He walked down the hall past his lab and continued to the front exit. As he rounded the corner, an elderly black man in a uniform looked startled for a moment but relaxed slightly when he saw Mark's badge and said, "Oh, you scared me there, mister. I didn't think anyone else was still here. It's not good to sneak up on an old man like that."

Mark, who had also been startled, regained his composure the best he could and replied, "I'm so sorry about that. I guess I must have been here while you guys switched shifts."

The old guard looked at Mark with some pity and said, "It's no good, working all the time, you know. You'll regret it one day. What good is working for money if you have no life outside of work to spend it on? Take an old man's advice about that."

Mark nodded and humored the old man. "Yes, I'm sure you are right about that. It's just for a little while. I don't plan on making a habit out of it."

The old man shook his head and said, "Son, it's all well and good to work hard for a better future, but what I've discovered in my considerable time in this world is this: If you want to know what your life is going to look like in the future, look around, because it's going to look pretty much like the present."

Mark frowned. How late was it, anyway? Too late for lectures on the philosophy of life, he knew that much.

Mark audibly exhaled and replied as humbly as he could, "I will give that some serious thought. Thank you. For now, though, I really must get home to bed."

"As you wish, sir," replied the guard. "Let me just scan your badge."

There was an audible beep from the hand-held scanner that the guard had whipped out with surprising speed.

"There, all done. You are clear to go." The guard spun the scanner and shoved it back into a holster that was directly beside a real gun. How funny would it have been if he had mixed them up? Not very, thought Mark.

Mark bowed his head slightly and went on his way. When he arrived at his car, Pryb was sleeping soundly in the back seat. Mark opened the door and gave him a sarcastic thumbs up before swiveling into the seat. He pinched the bridge of his nose for a second and then started the car. As he eased his way out of the parking lot and onto the highway, he thought about the old man's words. If you want to know what your future is going to be like, take a look at your present life. He shook his head and thought, God I hope not.

CHAPTER 25

———————— ▼ ————————

On Pryb's advisement, Mark let a full week elapse before attempting to use the suit again just to make sure that everything was copacetic.

Mark was as nervous as last time, but he was less nervous about taking the suit than he was about seeing Lisa again.

Pryb was not able to help Mark this time because he was on another one of his mysterious vacations. He had told Mark that he absolutely could not miss it. "Who has mandatory vacations?" reflected Mark.

Before leaving for parts unknown, Pryb had made further modifications to the security system. The outside cameras would now show sanitized images whenever Mark swiped to enter Plan A's lab. This meant that his walk to and from the car as well as his drive in and out of the facility would go unnoticed as long as no one witnessed it in person. That was a risk he would just have to take.

Mark was able to borrow the suit with ease this time around and he even remembered to bring a spare battery as well. The suit had an external battery port where one could be plugged in an emergency. Mark hated the styling of the suit, but he had to admit that some thought had at least gone into its usability.

After a thirty minute drive, he made the final turn onto Lisa's street. It was a cute middle-classed neighborhood. He could almost picture little kids playing noisily in their front yards, and then he instantly felt sorry for her. She must hate it here.

He watched for house numbers as he drove. 500. 502. 504. A lot with the charred remains of a house — still standing but just barely. 508. Damn, he missed it. He backed up and took a closer look at the charred house.

As he did, he remembered something that Pryb had said a few days earlier: "Hey, I've been thinking about your first meeting with Lisa. The thing is, since that defective suit only makes you half visible to each world, then that means that you are going to be half visible to Lisa, which is probably OK despite the fact that it will likely scare the daylights out of her, but you are also going to be half visible to whoever lives in that house in this world, right? But don't worry about it. I took steps."

Mark looked again at the wreckage of the house and reflected that his friend was something like a genie that gave you an infinite number of wishes, all of which likely to backfire. He shook his head.

Mark wondered briefly whether to park the car around the block, but in the end he felt that a car parked in front of an abandoned building was probably marginally less suspicious than a guy walking around the block in a marshmallow suit at eight in the evening.

Mark walked up to the front door and pushed the big, red button. Weirdly, there was only a hint of an unburnt house in front of him. He checked the suit, but the gauges all read normal. Strange.

He knocked at the door, feeling like he should at least have had a dozen roses in his hand as he did so. There was no answer. He knocked again, this time harder. He noticed with interest that his hand did not merge with the door as he did so. He tried slowly pushing at it and it did eventually go through, but only in the conventional sense in that it broke right through the charred door. Damn.

He checked the suit again. It said that it was working. He did notice, however, that one of the gauges did say that the phase ratio was at four percent, whatever that meant. He tried to remember what it had been at before but could not.

In the end, he gave up on knocking and found that the back door had been thoughtfully left unlocked — probably by Pryb. He entered and felt a slight twinge as he walked through the door. Once inside, he took a cautious look around. It looked really weird inside. It was mostly dark, as you would expect, but some parts were lit with a hazy light. The parts that were lit looked new and clean.

As far as he could tell, he was in the dining room. There was a china cabinet on his right that had a mirrored face to it. He glanced at his reflection. He was barely visible. On a hunch, he pushed the big, red button. He was now in near complete darkness. He reached out blindly in front of him but could feel nothing. They must have gutted the house after the fire, he thought. Well, that's good. At least I shouldn't be stumbling into things in the dark. Good old Pryb. He just wished that he knew what was wrong with the suit. Well, he came this far, might as well see if she is at home.

He pushed the button again, and the ghost of Lisa's house reappeared.

He followed the light into another room, a living room. Someone was sitting on the couch. Well, not someone exactly. The ghost of someone. The ghost of someone with straight, blonde hair. Could it really be her, wondered Mark with mounting excitement.

As he approached her from behind and slightly to the left, the ghost of a tabby cat sat up suddenly and focused its complete attention on Mark while its pupils dilated for better night vision.

The figure sitting on the couch noticed this and slowly turned around. To Mark's delight, it really was Lisa. He lifted one arm up and said, "Hello."

He had known, of course, that this is not his Lisa and was therefore expecting a scream, but none came. Lisa merely squinted in his general vicinity and then turned back around saying, "Stop freaking me out like that, Mark."

This caught Mark completely off guard and he instinctively apologized. Lisa, however, seemed to ignore him. "Hello?" he repeated. Nothing. He said it again and the cat hissed and ran away.

Lisa called out to the retreating cat, "What's gotten into you tonight, Mark?"

Mark thought about Lisa's choice to name her cat Mark. Interesting, he thought. There must have been a Mark-shaped hole in her life that needed filling. Another thought then occurred to him. I wonder if there is a real Mark in this world too? I really hope not. I'd hate to think that I'm poaching my own wife. That would be rather awkward.

It was becoming clear to Mark that communication was out, so he contented himself with merely watching Lisa for a few hours before giving up and leaving somewhat dejectedly out the back door.

He really needed to figure out what was wrong with the suit. Seeing a ghost Lisa and not being able to touch her or speak to her was almost worse than not being able to see her at all.

CHAPTER 26

---▼---

Mark took Brad's latest journal entry off the printer and settled into his chair to read it.

So, I was looking at the current trends in solar cells today, and I'm a little concerned. Most of the examples that I see are either blue or purple, but if you look at nature, anything that soaks up the sun's rays for energy is green. I think we're missing something important here. Just saying.

In other news, it took me 739 licks to get to the center of a Tootsie Pop. That's actually a hard metric to nail down. I mean, should the licks be evenly distributed? Are you disqualified if you put the whole thing in your mouth? When do you actually reach the center? Is it when any part of the core is open to the air, or does all the candy have to be dissolved all the way around? As a scientist, I need to know these things.

I'm thinking about renting some advertising space inside my journal. What kind of ads would you guys like to see? Let me know.

I think I've decided that I like cats more than dogs. I'm not sure exactly why yet. I'll get back to you on it.

In lab news today, we just confirmed our
suspicions about the Mark I suit's
feasibility, which is that it basically
sucks when taken away from the lab.

Mark laughed to himself and said, "You got that right." He
continued reading.

The white coats say that this was to be
expected and has something to do with the
control signal lag between central command
and the suit. They are now working on a
smaller version of the control circuitry
with the hope of integrating it into a new
suit in order to eliminate this problem. The
hope is that this will be completed in under
two months. In the meantime, they think they
can raise the current synchronization rate a
bit, but the process won't be perfected
until the Mark II is ready. For now, they've
got plenty of stupid experiments for me to
try near the lab using the old suit. Hooray
for me.

Personally, I can't wait for the new suit.
Whatever it's like, it has to be better than
this current one. This one really kicks me
in the machismo every time I have to wear
it. Thank God this is a secret project — I'd
hate to have to take press photos wearing
that thing. Seriously, get to work you guys.

I think that about covers all new
discoveries for today. No, wait, I did also
discover how to cure cancer today. The
secret is to... ah, never mind, I can tell
you guys aren't interested. Talk to you
tomorrow.

Mark fed the paper into his shredder and went to bed.

CHAPTER 27

—————— ▼ ——————

Mark returned to Lisa's house a few days later wearing the same Marshmallow suit as before. He had debated with himself over the pointlessness of visiting her without being able to actually interact with her, but in the end his loneliness had won the argument.

He was inside the burnt remains of someone's home, sitting on a cinder block while trying to work up the courage to visit her again. He felt almost like a teen who was about to go on a first date. What if she sees him? What should he say? How do I explain a concept like "I've come from another dimension to visit you because you are a parallel version of my departed wife and I miss her more than life itself," while only being able to wave my hands around?

He'd have to settle for being as non-threatening as he could, and hopefully get her used to the idea of his presence so that by the time he actually could communicate meaningfully with her, she would be well beyond the screaming and running away stage.

With that sketchy plan in mind, Mark walked to where the kitchen should be and flicked over to her world. Just as before, the suit was majorly out of synchronization, which meant that he was mostly still present in World(0), and barely present in World(+1).

He looked around at the ghost of Lisa's kitchen. He waved his hand experimentally through the counter top. He could feel only the slightest resistance, as he had expected.

Instead of going directly to the living room where Lisa was likely to be, he decided to investigate the house a little more. With any luck, he might gain some insight into this other Lisa's life.

He had to admit to himself that he felt rather creepy at this point. Not creepy as in scary, but creepy as in acting like a creep. It did not feel right to be sneaking around someone's house at night, even if in another world he had known that someone for well over half his life.

Feeling conflicted, he debated on whether to keep snooping, but in the end he decided to do so — but he would feel really bad about it, so that would be OK.

Mark walked down the hallway and into the bedroom. The door had been closed but that didn't matter much to him. Closed doors were something that happened to other people.

There was a light by the bed that was on some sort of sensor that turned it on at dusk. It was on now. Mark studied it and said, "Hmm, yes, that seems like her. That would save her the trouble of climbing over the bed to turn on the small light, then climbing back over to turn out the main light. Doing all that climbing before bed would surely wake a person up again. And it never would have occurred to her to move the lamp to the other side of the bed. He continued to survey the room.

From what he could see of the ghostly room, it appeared to be very tidy. He looked at the dresser. On top of it were a few little girly knick knacks and a badge with her picture on it. The badge read "Sisyphus Laboratories". Mark frowned at the name. It sounded like a place that studied venereal diseases. No, wait, he thought. Isn't that the Greek guy who had to keep rolling a huge boulder uphill every day, only to watch it roll back down again just inches from the top, for all eternity? Well, I guess science can feel like that sometimes, but I'm still not too sure about the name.

He walked over to the nightstand. He could see no pictures on top of it beyond one of her parents. He wasn't sure what he would have done had he seen one of himself. If it came to that, he wasn't sure what he would have done had he seen one of any man. Part of him was relieved, but a larger part felt sorry for her. She must be lonely.

He suddenly did not feel like snooping anymore. Actually, to be more specific, he suddenly felt like seeing Lisa. He left the bedroom and walked back down the hallway.

Lisa was in the living room again this evening watching the Discovery channel with her cat. Mark felt so bad for her sitting there all alone in the dark. He instinctively came up behind her and gave her a gentle hug. He could feel the slight pressure of her body and a tingle as her cheek touched his. Lisa screamed.

Her cat hissed. Mark slammed the big, red button.

Now fully back in World(0), Mark said, "Damn."

CHAPTER 28

▼

Mark settled back in his chair with the latest printout. He coughed a couple of times and then began to read it.

There has been a major breakthrough today. I'm very excited. I've been waiting for this moment for weeks. Sally has finally written back! She wrote "I miss you Thomas. Meet me here next Thursday." Isn't that wonderful? I'm a trans-dimensional match maker!

As if that weren't exciting enough, I've also discovered that I like Cheez Whiz. No, it's the god's honest truth. Give it a try sometime. Really.

On a darker note, someone has been pulling childish pranks at work and I'm being blamed. I find this completely unfair. I could handle being scolded if it were really me, but it isn't so I'm very annoyed.

On the other hand, I do have to admit that the pranks are definitely my style. I mean, just yesterday someone switched the hot and cold water on all the sinks in the main restroom. And I'm not talking about just switching the H and C labels here, I'm talking about taking hours of time to actually reroute the plumbing. Marvelous. My hat is off to whomever is doing it. I just wish that I wasn't the one getting the blame for it. What a bastard.

I suppose I should mention a little something about the experiments today if only for the look of the thing. Today we tried to bring material from our world into World(+1) and leave it in there. We tried it with a geranium plant because A) it is organic and B) we found some in the reception area.

The white coats had grafted on a special specimen compartment to my suit for the occasion. If it weren't already bad enough having to dress like a marshmallow, now they gave me a fanny pack. I swear this is retribution for the pranks that I'm being unjustly accused of perpetrating. Anyway, the compartment was rigged so that I could open it with a push of a button on my sleeve and it would dump the contents on its own.

The experiment was conducted inside the courtyard. The hope was that if it survived, then I could plant it out there on World(+1) and would study it in the following weeks to see if it survived.

This, as it turned out, was a bit too ambitious. When I opened the door to the compartment and allowed the flower to fall out, it turned to fine powder and a few fibrous shreds of violet and green, all of which appeared back in World(0). This makes me very glad that one of the white coats had stopped me from taking a leak the other day while the suit was still active. Very, very glad.

Needless to say, the white coats are

```
interested in this result but the green
shirts are angry about it because it
seriously delays their plans to pillage
another dimension. Score one for science,
then.
```

Mark shredded the journal entry with a frown on his face. It sounded like he would be imprisoned inside that silly suit whenever he visited Lisa. That's going to get old fast, he thought.

CHAPTER 29

---▼---

Tonight, Lisa was on the couch in the dimly-lit living room staring blearily at the TV yet again. She was watching some sort of horrible reality TV show. Mark saw it and frowned. This was not like the Lisa he had known, who would rather have eaten her own eyeballs over watching such garbage. Perhaps this shows just how devastating an effect loneliness can have on a person.

Mark walked beside the couch and reached out for the remote control. The other Mark — the feline one — noticed this and hissed. The cat jumped off Lisa's lap, causing Lisa to jump too. She accidentally knocked the TV remote off the side table where it landed out of her view beside the couch.

While Lisa was chastising the cat, Mark crouched down and examined the remote. He found the channel button and attempted to press it. His finger passed through it, as expected. This time he did it very quickly. There was just enough resistance to activate the button. Thanks to the recent modifications done by the white coats, the suit was now at eight percent synchronization. This meant that he could now see Lisa a little better and also interact with her world a little more.

Lisa blinked at the TV in surprise as it cycled through the channels on its own. She looked for the remote on the side table but it was gone. She thought maybe it had wedged between the couch cushions with its channel button depressed, so she stood up to investigate. The channel stopped changing. OK, so that was it, she thought.

She removed the cushions one-by-one but found no sign of the remote. While she was replacing the last cushion and contemplating turning on the light to have a better look, she saw the remote lying on the floor beside the couch. She tilted her head at it, and then picked it up.

With her finger hovering over the channel button, she stopped herself from pressing it because she saw a cute, little animal face on the TV screen. The show was about meerkats, apparently, and it had been filmed in a style that was reminiscent of a reality show in that the little critters were filmed 24/7 in their natural habitat. Each of the meerkats had names and unique personalities. They even had a little society, in fact, with rules and a social hierarchy. It was very interesting so she left it on.

Suddenly she felt a presence beside her. She jerked her head to the left to see what it was. To her amazement, she could just make out the outline of a white blobby figure that was not so much sitting on the couch as through it. It looked vaguely annoyed. She was just about to pull away from it when it suddenly disappeared.

Now back fully in his world, Mark cursed under his breath as he gathered up pieces of rubble to stack up for him to sit on. He placed them exactly at the location of Lisa's couch in the other world and activated the suit again.

Lisa froze when she saw the strange white blob rematerialize in front of the couch and just to the left of her. She watched as it gingerly sat down on the couch next to her. It seemed calmer now and was sitting on the cushion this time, not through it. Her heart stopped when it turned its featureless face towards hers. It then gave her a self-satisfied nod that was so endearing that it made her giggle. "Good for you," she said. It was obviously happy that it could sit on the couch.

Lisa wondered what to do next. She wondered if she should try to touch it. It seemed friendly, almost timid, but she did not wish to scare it off — this was just too amazing. She decided not to touch it, but she did shift ever so slightly closer to it. The ghost, in turn, gave her another small nod and then turned its attention to the TV.

Lisa, not knowing what else to do, watched along with it. She noticed that it would shake during the funny parts, almost as if it were laughing along with her. She started to talk out loud to it, not saying much in particular, mainly relaying her thoughts and observations on the show. This seemed to make the blob happy. She found that it would even nod or shake its head when she asked it yes or no questions.

After a while, they were sitting so close that they were touching. She could actually feel a little pressure from its existence. A few times she thought that she heard it speak, but it was so faint that she could not make out what it was saying.

They continued watching TV after that in silence. Her eyes started to get heavy. She thought she felt it gently stroking her hair as she slowly fell asleep.

The next morning, Lisa woke up on the couch all alone. She suddenly felt a great emptiness when she realized that it had all been a dream. However, in his own world, Mark woke up on top of the world with the knowledge that it had been real.

CHAPTER 30

▼

Mark was sitting in his usual spot at the back of the cafeteria. He was there a little earlier than usual today and the place was very crowded so he was sharing a table with two other employees. Their badges indicated that they were from Plan B.

Mark usually came to the cafeteria at odd hours with the hope of being left alone, but this somehow always backfired — perhaps because he then stood out in the nearly empty room. Inevitably someone he knew would spot him while stumbling in for a snack and would feel it was somehow rude not to converse with him.

So today his plan was to come during the busiest part of the day with the hope that he would just be background noise to the chaos of the lunch hour. When Brad sat down across from him five minutes later, he knew that he had failed again.

Brad waved his hand as he sat down and said, "Hey, brother. Looks like you got hungry early today too. I don't blame you since it's pizza day."

Mark replied, "Yes, well, no one makes a pizza quite like Mario."

Brad took a bite of his pizza and chewed thoughtfully. "True," he replied. "They have the algorithms tuned just perfect. I hear that Mario even samples the acidity of the sauce and the alkalinity of the cheese and adjusts its ratios for perfect harmony."

"Personally," replied Mark, "I think it's the fake mustache that does the trick." He took another bite of his own slice.

The two ate in silence for a moment and then Brad asked, "So, how are your lab rats doing?"

Mark finished chewing and answered, "Oh, those guys — they're doing alright. We finally convinced the one guy that it wasn't our fault that his girlfriend got pregnant even though, in his words, the treatments have been making him as randy as a rabbit."

"It's probably not a good idea to shake hands with him, then."

Mark made a face. "He does disappear into the bathroom a lot. Anyway, besides dealing with their mental issues, they are all doing well. Physically they seem pretty solid."

Brad leaned closer and asked, "Has anyone developed any latent superpowers, yet?"

"You mean, apart from being randy as a rabbit? No, not that we've seen. Although, I have to say that they do have superhuman strength and stamina now. I certainly wouldn't want to fight with them," explained Mark.

Brad smirked and said, "It doesn't sound like fighting is what's on their minds."

"Ha-ha," replied Mark. "That's just the one guy, thank you very much."

"Well, with all that stamina, it's no wonder that he..."

Mark interrupted, "Yes, yes. Anyway, how's your project going? In a vague and nonspecific manner, of course."

Brad answered, "Well, vaguely pretty good, although I'm getting sort of bored. It seems like... how do I put this non-specifically... like they are holding back. Like not much progress has been made recently but somehow they all seem excited about something. I'm not sure what to make of it."

"Odd," observed Mark.

"Too right. Anyway, other than that, things are progressing. How are things with you and Tammy?"

Mark was just about to take a bite of his pizza but instead froze there for a moment with his mouth open. His eyes glanced over at the other two at the table and mentally toned down what he was about to say.

"There isn't any me and Tammy. She still hints at getting together, but she hasn't been all that bad. Honestly, she is pretty decent company."

"Yeah, right," replied Brad. "That's why you keep randomizing your lunch period."

Mark made a face at him.

Brad suddenly looked thoughtful and said, "Oh, by the way, before I forget, watch out when you open your locker. The phantom prankster filled them up with chocolate puddings that he stole from the pantry."

Mark was just about to say, "Tammy must be in heaven," when he remembered the others at the table and held it in.

Brad laughed at the face Mark made and said, "I know exactly what you were about to say."

Mark cleared his throat and said, "At any rate, thanks for the warning — although I don't seem to be getting pranked for some reason. I wonder why that is?" He looked at Brad suspiciously.

Brad replied, "Why indeed," and returned the look.

Mark suddenly looked affronted. "You don't think it's me, do you?"

Brad replied, "Who could say? It would explain why it isn't happening to you. At any rate, we can definitely rule out one person now."

Mark looked puzzled and asked, "Who?"

Brad smirked and said, "Tammy — there is no way she would waste all that chocolate pudding."

CHAPTER 31

▼

In World(+1), Lisa sighed as she tidied up her house ahead of her accountant's arrival. She was very torn. On one hand, the ghost had visited her a few more times over the course of the last two weeks and they seemed to be getting along well together, considering the circumstances. On the other hand, when looked at it objectively, dating a ghost was not a normal thing to do. Some might even call it creepy. And her accountant was a pretty cute guy in a shy and dorky kind of way. Not to mention, he was also a solid human being rather than a fuzzy white blob, and a woman has needs.

In World(0), Mark sighed as he prepared to visit Lisa once again. He both loved and loathed the visits. On the one hand, it was great to get to see Lisa again and somewhat interact with her, but on the other hand the interaction was very minimal with no real sense of touch or communication. It was frustrating and depressing. He prayed every day that the white coats would hurry up and improve the technology, but in the meantime he was limited to these awkward encounters, so he had to take what he could get.

He flicked into World(+1) a little way away from Lisa's couch. It was about eight o'clock so he knew she would be settling in to watch some television. Only she wasn't there.

He heard laughter coming from the kitchen — both Lisa's and some unknown male's laughter. Mark frowned and walked to the kitchen to investigate.

Lisa was sitting at the kitchen table with... Pryb?!? He called out, "Pryb, you bastard, what the heck are you doing here?" However, no one heard him.

On second glance, maybe it was not Pryb. He had Pryb's face, no doubt about that, but this was a Pryb with some hair; a

Pryb with a skinnier frame and no tattoos; a Pryb doing accounting instead of international espionage; a Pryb, in fact, that was nothing at all like the Pryb he knew.

The kitchen table was scattered with paperwork and receipts. Pryb was talking about itemized deductions while Lisa was... flirting with him. Mark blinked hard. No, she was definitely flirting — cracking jokes and playfully touching him on the arm while laughing at the awful jokes he told in return. It was sickening. Mark took a swing at him.

The accountant's comb-over was tousled by Mark's blow, which briefly revealed his balding head before he quickly smoothed it back into position with his hand. Lisa pretended not to have noticed and said, "It's a bit breezy in here, isn't it?" She walked over to the open kitchen window and shut it.

No one seemed to notice Mark. The bright lights and white walls of the kitchen must have rendered him invisible.

The accountant, now slightly flustered, snapped open the clasps of his briefcase and opened it. He then pulled out a can of Pringles potato chips and offered some to Lisa, but she declined with a wave of her hand.

It really is Pryb, thought Mark while watching the man eat the potato chips. I'm looking at Pryb from World(+1). So in this world he's an accountant? How strange. Why would he be so different here? He stared blankly at the Pringles can while deep in thought.

It was at that moment that Mark got an idea. It was so simple, wasn't it? Why hadn't he thought of it before?

He flicked back into World(0) and quickly removed the suit. Now in his normal clothes, he drove around the block to the local convenience store and bought a can of Pringles.

He then raced back to the abandoned home and searched for a nail in the rubble. He used the nail to perforate the side of the Pringles can after hastily dumping its contents on the lawn out back.

Now he quickly changed back into the suit and jammed the Pringles can over the antenna on his helmet that linked him to the main computer back at the lab. With any luck, this should boost his signal just like it did for the wifi signal back home.

He flicked the switch. Lisa's apartment reappeared, but it was just as insubstantial as before.

Lisa did not appear to be in the room. The accountant, however, was. Mark was standing right beside him.

Mark grabbed onto the Pringles can with one hand to steady it. He scolded himself for not buying some tape while he was at the store. Oh well. He turned his head this way and that, trying to align the can in the direction of the lab. By walking around to the other side of the accountant and bending his neck in a funny angle, he was able to do it.

Suddenly, a blobby white apparition appeared just beside the accountant. The apparition had one red horn, which it seemed to be tugging at in some sort of act of self torture. Its head was bent nearly ninety degrees sideways. The accountant wet his pants and then ran out of the house in embarrassment and fear.

Mark called out, "Lisa! Lisa! It's me. Can you hear me?" and then turned his head slightly to see if she was coming. The Pringles can knocked into the kitchen's hanging lamp and dislodged from his helmet. Mark said, "Oh hell," and then disappeared from World(+1) just as Lisa was running into the kitchen to investigate the voice.

Lisa thought she saw her ghost friend for the merest fraction of a second. Was that him that called to her? She looked around frantically but no one was there. The accountant was gone, but his paperwork was still there. So was a faint smell of urine. She wrinkled her nose and continued to look around the house for signs of anyone or any ghost, but found none.

Meanwhile, back in World(0), Mark had just accidentally stepped on the Pringles can and had crushed it. He swore — cursing the universe and everyone in it for conspiring to make his life so difficult.

After a while he calmed down and tried to look on the bright side. Firstly, dorky Pryb was not likely to come calling on Lisa again, and secondly, he now had a viable way to project himself more fully into World(+1). With that knowledge, Mark smiled while he packed up his things and returned to the lab. Things were finally going to get better for him, he just knew it.

CHAPTER 32

---▼---

The Brad in World(-1) put on the Flicker suit and giggled. He had all sorts of fun planned for tonight. During the day, the white coats were giving him boring things to do like trying to collect soil samples from the courtyard or some very restrictive surveillance of the local town's inhabitants in the next world. However, they were not allowing him to interact with anyone, which was boring.

Now that it was nighttime, however, it was his turn to shine. The security at the lab seemed surprisingly lax. He had already figured out a way to fool the computer into ignoring his presence after hours, so now he had carte blanche access to the suit and was looking forward to some mischief.

He knew that in his own world there were cameras in the Plan A lab, but none in the rest of the building. He had been able to rig the security system to freeze the camera image whenever he was in the lab after hours, but he had no way of doing the same in the next world. This meant that he had to stay out of his lab when he was in the next world, otherwise the cameras there would spot him and the jig would be up.

To this end, he opened the door and cautiously looked out into the hallway. No one was there, as it should have been. He quickly put on his helmet, stepped outside the room, and flicked over to the next world.

This was not his first trip over by any means. Brad had been doing this for several weeks now — popping over to the next world and pulling some hijinks. It was stress relief for him.

Interestingly enough, it was not originally his idea to steal the suit for a joy ride. He actually got the idea from Mark.

Mark had not realized it, but Brad had been working late on the very same night he had stolen the suit for the first time.

Brad had left the bathroom just in time to see Mark putting on the helmet of the suit and gingerly walking through the wall with it. Brad never broached the subject with Mark out of fear of getting him in trouble if someone overheard.

Unfortunately, Brad had noticed a drastic change in Mark's demeanor shortly after that night. He had looked as if all the meaning in his life had been ripped out from his soul. He even quit the company a few days later. And a week after that, he was found dead at the bottom of a cliff. Officially, it had been ruled as a hiking accident, but Brad suspected otherwise.

All the same, the prospect of having his soul ripped out from his body never stopped a test pilot like Brad. To the contrary, it only piqued his curiosity even more and he began his unsupervised trips to the next world.

It took Brad a couple of trips before he figured out what had happened to Mark. This had come not so much as a result of patient detective work as it had from Brad being able to relax his mind and seriously think things through. Unfortunately for those around him, Brad's main form of relaxation was by practical joking.

One day while Brad was re-plumbing the bathroom sinks in the next world for a laugh, he had figured things out. His reasoning went like this: Mark had been a total wreck after his wife had died, so much so that he had to take an extended leave of absence. After that, he suddenly returned with an air of unwavering determination about his person and a sudden interest in the Flicker Project. Why? The answer was simple when he thought about it. Mark must have hoped to see his wife again in the next world.

Brad had then done some light detective work and discovered what Mark must have also inevitably discovered — that the Lisa in the next world was also dead. Mark therefore had no hope of seeing her again, had become despondent, and had killed himself. That much was clear now. If only he had realized it sooner then he might have been able to talk him out of it.

CHAPTER 33

---▼---

"Jesus, Mary and Joseph, and little baby Jesus! What the hell were you thinking breaking into the lab so many times while I was gone? Are you thick or what? What are you laughing at?"

Mark was trying to stop his laughter, but the more he tried the more he laughed harder.

"Would you like me to thump you? Would that help? I'll do it as a friend if you think it will help. Now tell me what's so damn funny?"

Mark tried to catch his breath. "It's just..." <laughter> "...I can't stop..." <laughter> "...picturing you with a comb-over." <Raucous laughter>

Pryb raised a fist and held it over Mark's head. Mark held his palm up and said, "OK, OK." <Giggle> "I'm done." <Giggle> <Snigger>

Eventually Mark's laughter sputtered to an end. He wiped away a tear and said, "I'm sorry, but I really needed that."

"Are you on drugs?" questioned Pryb.

Mark shook his head and explained to Pryb about the accountant in World(+1).

"Well I'll be the son of a motherless goat," replied Pryb after hearing it.

"You've got some colorful phrases, Pryb."

"Must be from my Irish upbringing."

"I thought you were Polish?"

Pryb shrugged. "I'm Irish on Tuesdays." He grinned.

Mark shook his head. "And you think I'm the one on drugs."

Pryb waved his hand dismissively. "Yeah, well anyway, what's that mutton-headed test pilot have to say today?"

"I thought you liked Brad," questioned Mark.

"I do. I guess I have a thing for mutton-heads. Must be why I like you so much. Although I've always thought of you as more of a chowder-head."

Mark squinted at his friend for a moment and then took the latest printout and began to read it.

Well here's a thing. I'm not even sure where to start. Do you want the good news first or the bad? Let me just flip a coin here for your answer... It's heads. That's the good news. Well, the good news is that I'm no longer suspected of being the phantom prankster. The bad news is that good old Steve has had Tammy and the creepy-ass creeps from Plan B spy on me for the last several months. It really makes me shudder when I think about it. Apparently it was 24-hour surveillance. Lord knows what they saw me doing. No wonder Tammy has been giving me that Cheshire Cat look every time we pass by each other. I feel so violated.

But, as I said, they no longer believe that I did the pranks and I'm assured that the surveillance has been lifted. The evidence points to the test pilot from World(-1) (me but not me) as the culprit. No wonder I liked that cat's style so much.

Anyway, because of that suspicion, the security of the whole building will be drastically overhauled. In fact, they plan on closing down the entire facility next Monday for a week while they make the changes. Steve also thought about suspending overtime as well, but then I raised the point that it would be better to have more people to keep an eye out than less at a time like this, so he let it be for now. However, overtime may be indefinitely suspended after the new security measures are in place. Not that I care since I'm a straight nine-to-fiver. Er, OK, ten-to-three'er.

Let's see... What else? Oh, right! Apparently the new Mark II suit has been ready for several weeks but the white coats have been keeping it from me as a sort of punishment for the practical jokes they thought I've been perpetrating. No love, I tell you.

Oh, but this new suit is way cool. It's more or less skin tight and dark metallic gray. Very sexy. It's like a straight up super hero suit — only sadly still without a cape.

Unfortunately, I do have to continue to wear a bulky helmet since the white coats are not really sure what would happen if I were to breathe air from World(+1) and then return to this one. Something about possible vacuums in my lungs and arteries. Probably not good at any rate. So, I put up with the helmet in the name of safety. At least the marshmallow suit is gone, gone, gone!

Oh, and hey, not only is this new suit much less bulky, but it is also (supposedly) capable of full synchronization. And it's able to do so without the support of the lab's computer. What this means in layman's terms is that I'll be able to be fully present in World(+1) with no limitation on my distance from the lab. Presumably this is how my alter ego from World(-1) has been able to perpetrate his heinous slander of my otherwise flawless character over the last few weeks. Apparently his team trusted him with the new suit at an earlier time. Good for him. But if I ever catch him here, I'm

still going to kick him straight in the fork
— believe it.

Mark stopped reading and oscillated between looking happy and worried.

"What's up?" asked Pryb, noticing this.

"Well, you heard what I just read. There's a new suit that will let me interact more with Lisa. I'll be able to touch her and talk to her now. But I'm worried about the new security." He bit his thumb nail. "I'd like to take the old suit out one last time before the new security kicks in. I have an idea to make it work better. I'll be able to talk with Lisa if it works. At least this way I can explain the situation and say goodbye if I can't figure out a way past the new security."

Pryb was going to argue but he recognized that determined look in his friend's eyes and reconsidered. Instead, he simply gave Mark a nod of agreement.

CHAPTER 34

Lisa paced around her house very much like how a caged cougar will pace around the perimeter of its confines. She also felt just as restless. The trouble was, the more she tried not to think about what was bothering her, the more she thought about it, and the more it bothered her.

Deep inside, she knew why she was pacing the house. She was waiting for him. This made her really question her sanity. Was she really so lonely that she actually looked forward to the company of a ghost? Apparently so.

He hadn't appeared for several days now. Lisa was wondering why. As far as she could tell, they had parted amiably the last time they had met. Although, now that she thought about it, there was that weird disturbance in the kitchen a few nights ago. She had sworn she had heard a voice call out to her from the kitchen and it wasn't the voice of her accountant. Maybe that was it. Could he have been jealous? Maybe he's mad at me now?

She glanced at the clock. It was past the time that he would normally appear. She frowned, walked over to her cell phone, and dialed her accountant. No answer, again. She really wanted to know what had happened in the kitchen that night, but he seemed to be dodging her calls. And now the ghost was gone too. Somehow she had managed to ruin even those two sad promises of romance. How pathetic was that?

She wandered out into her back yard. The garden was there, and it looked a little weedy. Well, she could at least do something about that.

She worked one full row of the garden, head down and concentrating fully on the mindless tedium of weeding while lit by a single spotlight mounted just under the roof of the house.

She was halfway done with the next row when she noticed something odd — the weeds were already pulled out for the remainder of the row. She looked left and right. The balance of the garden was also done. The hair on the back of her neck bristled.

A voice behind her said, "I couldn't just stand here and not help you."

She spun around and screamed.

A semi transparent white blob held up its hands in a gesture of harmlessness and said, "Sorry. Sorry. It's OK. It's me. You call me Blobby Bob. Remember? My real name is Mark, by the way. I'm so glad to finally be able to talk to you."

Lisa gibbered. She sheepishly pointed toward Mark and hesitantly said, "Y...you." She gibbered some more. Then she looked puzzled. Her finger now pointed at Mark's head. She said with much less hesitancy and almost a hint of humor, "What the hell is that on your head?" She let a dainty giggle escape her mouth and then covered it in embarrassment.

Mark smiled. Was Lisa always this adorable? At any rate, he knew exactly what she was pointing at and exactly how stupid it must look. He smiled and replied, "This is a very delicate and essential piece of scientific equipment, I'll have you know. The fact that it resembles a Pringles can on a camera gimbal that has been duct taped to my helmet is purely coincidental."

Lisa let her laughter escape freely now. Mark laughed a little too before explaining, "It's a long story, but this really is essential in allowing me to see you properly like this, and to talk to you. I... I imagine you have a few questions for me."

Lisa let out a single hollow laugh and said, "You think? I'm not even sure where to begin. How about you just tell me everything. I guess you can start with what the hell you are. Now that I can see you better, I'm guessing you aren't a ghost. Maybe a space man? Or the ghost of a space man from a planet of obese marshmallow people? At the very least, I see from the writing on your chest that you claim to be a big aardvark, but I have my doubts about that."

Mark laughed again and mumbled, "God I missed you."

"What?" asked Lisa.

"Sorry. Let me try to explain. I've been waiting for this moment for a while, but now that it's here I'm terrified of screwing it up."

"Just tell me the truth. If you want to get along with me at all, then you must always tell me the truth."

"Ah," said Mark, "So you are a lot like her."

"Who?"

"Let me start from the beginning. Firstly, my name is Mark. I'm a human being — a living one. And... well, this is where it gets hard to believe, but bear with me... I'm from another world. Er, no, that's misleading. Another dimension, I guess would be the better way to put it. Do you believe me so far?"

Lisa furrowed her brow. "Well, let's just say that I have no contradictory evidence at this point. Please proceed."

Mark smiled. She was definitely like his Lisa, he thought. "Good. OK. So, as you can see, I'm wearing this stupid marshmallow suit. It's a Mark I prototype, which I'm sure you can tell by its looks. It lets me project myself into your world, but it is imperfect so I'm also about fifty percent back in my world as well."

Lisa thought about this.

Mark noticed her silence and asked, "Did I say something wrong?"

Lisa held up a hand to silence him. Mark had seen that gesture plenty of times before and knew to stop talking.

After another few seconds Lisa asked, "So is there another me in your world that is simultaneously talking to you right now?"

This startled Mark for a second, both because of her perceptiveness but also at the realization that by asking it she had just moved up his timetable of when he was going to finally admit why he was there. He saw Lisa studying his face through his visor.

Lisa asked, "Was that OK to ask? You look... pained."

Mark gave her a smile tinged with sadness and answered, "Yes. Perfectly fine. I just... wasn't quite expecting the conversation to become serious so soon."

"Ah," said Lisa with a nod, "So we've reached that point in the conversation, have we? The point where you admit that you've been spying on me for a long time now, peeping at me from some other dimension, and now finally you are here to profess your undying love for me while wearing a marshmallow suit with a rotating Pringles can on your head."

Mark laughed so hard that he folded over slightly, which caused a disruption in his signal, which in turn caused him to flicker away and then reappear. He noticed this and attempted to regain his composure.

He paused to collect his thoughts and made a start at a few sentences before finally saying, "Not quite right, and not quite that creepy, but perhaps still creepy in some respects."

Lisa tilted her head. "Go on."

Mark looked up for a second and then said, "To answer your question from before, no, I am not also speaking to another Lisa right now in my world. And you see, that is sort of the problem. Back in my world, I met you, that is, I met another you, a Lisa from my world, when I was only ten years old. We were inseparable from that point on." Mark's voice became a little strangled at this point and he continued, "Recently we were married and moved in together. We were blissfully happy. Well, at first. Work started getting in the way, as it sometimes does, but anyway, that's beside the point. The point is, she's gone now. She died in a car accident."

Lisa's face went white and her mouth made an almost perfect "O".

Mark continued, "So, needless to say, I was devastated. I nearly killed myself from malnutrition, but before that happened, I had an epiphany. I figured out a way to see you again. This crazy suit is from my work." Mark lifted the arms in demonstration. "I thought, maybe, just maybe, you might be alive in this world. And I was right." He stopped talking to get a read on Lisa's reaction.

At first she remained frozen while she processed all of this, but eventually she shook her head slightly and gave Mark a bittersweet smile in return. Her eyes looked a little glassy. Mark's did too. Finally, she said, "I don't find that creepy at all, Mark. It's all so tragic. You poor man." She paused, as if deciding whether she should say what was coming next. She inhaled and decided to say it. "But you know, I can never be her. I don't have her same memories. I haven't known you more than a few weeks of awkwardly sitting beside you on the couch. I haven't had her life."

Mark nodded. "Yes. I... I'm well aware of that. I'm not sure what I expected. I guess I always knew that you would be different. But I wanted to see her again so badly and this was the only thing I could think of to do. I'm sorry. This is... It's really not fair to you, is it? I'm... I... I should probably go. This was a mistake. I'm sorry."

"No, wait!" exclaimed Lisa, much to the shock of both of

them. Lisa covered her mouth momentarily in embarrassment. After she had recovered, she said more softly, "Wait. Please don't go. I completely get how weird this is. Believe me, I get it. But, if it is OK with you, I'd like you to keep visiting. I don't know why, but I feel like we are supposed to be together. Is that weird?" She furrowed her brow again and asked rhetorically, "Do you suppose there is another Mark running around in this world and I just never met him?"

Mark interrupted her by saying, "If there is another Mark here, then I'd track him down and date him if I were you. I bet he's an awesome guy." Mark gave her a thumbs up.

Lisa shook her head. "Yeah, right. I'll start by looking in all the nearby mental wards, shall I?"

Mark smiled. "That would probably be a safe bet. In all seriousness, though, if you don't mind, I would like to know what happened to me in this world. If you have the time, I would really, really appreciate it if you could research that for me."

Lisa thought about this then answered, "Sure. But don't blame me if I run away with him, OK? After all, I'm sure he's bound to be a little less marshmallowy than you." She poked his suit. To her surprise, her finger went through the suit. It felt like poking a pudding. Mark shivered.

"Please don't do that again," Mark said slowly and deliberately.

Lisa looked at her finger. She sniffed it.

Mark made a face at her and said, "It's a bit complicated, but since I'm here and not here at the same time, I'm not entirely solid. In fact, I've been stealing the suit by simply walking through the wall with it."

"Seems a bit of a design flaw," replied Lisa.

Mark shrugged. "Well, it is a prototype after all. Speaking of which, I have to tell you this before I run out of time. I have limited battery power on this thing, after all. Anyway, there is a new suit, the Mark II, which is now ready for testing. Only, the thing is, they are also stepping up the security at the lab, and as you might have guessed, I'm not exactly supposed to be taking this out for a joy ride at night. So, well, I'm not sure how long it will be before I can see you next. I'll try to make it fast but I have to be careful. My guess is less than a month. But look, the new suit will be form fitting so no more Blobby Bob. And I'll be fully here, so no more poking your finger through my spleen. That's good, right?"

Lisa nodded. "Yes. Yes, it sounds good. Just, be careful. It's cute that you want to hurry back and see me, but I'll be fine. I'd rather you be safe. In the meantime, I'll see what I can find out about the Mark from this world. Uh... you might want to tell me your last name."

Mark gave her all the information he could think of to help her find the other Mark.

Mark looked at the power gauge on his arm. He had to get going. He smiled at Lisa and said, "Well, I really have to get going. My power is getting low. I need some to walk back into the lab." He sighed and continued, "This might be goodbye. If it is, I just want to say that it was a pleasure to meet you, and even though you are not my Lisa, I think you are still a wonderful woman. If you do happen to find your Mark here, and you two do hit it off, just do me one favor. If he starts working a little too hard and it seems like he's neglecting you, cut him a little slack. He really does intend to put an end to it. My Lisa ran out of patience in the end. Anyway, I've got to go now. See you around."

Before Lisa could reply, Mark vanished. In her mind's eye, she could still see him standing there, smiling at her with tears in his eyes. She started to cry as well.

CHAPTER 35

Mark hurried through the wall as fast as he could before the suit's battery power could give out. He emerged on the inside of the lab folded over in pain. He quickly removed his helmet and was standing there alternating between panting from exhaustion and coughing up blood.

He saw the blood splatter on the ground and frowned at it. He quickly removed the Mark I suit and left it as a crumpled heap on the floor while he went to the medical room to find alcohol and gauze, which he hoped would be useful in cleaning up the blood.

When Mark was halfway to the room, the door to the lab suddenly opened. Silhouetted by the hallway lights was the unmistakable profile of Brad. He was wearing a silver suit. He saw Mark and froze. Mark saw him and froze.

Time passed.

Mark guiltily looked back at the crumpled suit behind him and then back at Brad again. He bit his lip for a second and then said, "Hi."

Brad considered this.

Time passed.

"Hi," he replied.

At this point the wheels inside both of their heads began spinning as if fueled by hamsters on amphetamines as each man sought for a plausible reason why they were doing what they were doing.

Mark was milliseconds away from saying, "OK, you caught me," when he was preempted by Brad, who was looking uncharacteristically rattled.

Brad took a few steps closer to Mark while he said, "Is it really you? Let me get a good look at you." He took a few more steps and was now about a foot away from Mark, studying his face in worrying detail.

Mark took a step back.

"Umm..." he replied.

Brad seemed to collect himself and said. "Sorry, it's just that where I come from, you're dead."

Mark squinted at him while taking another step back. Then he said, "Where you come from? Ah. I see. You're from World(-1), right?"

Brad nodded. He looked puzzled and asked, "Why aren't you dead? The Mark that I knew just offed himself in the woods. Dude took a dive over a cliff. I think he was distraught after losing his girl. Does that mean she's still alive here?"

Mark frowned and shook his head.

Brad turned his head to the side and peered at Mark out of the corner of his eyes. "Ah. Well, my Mark stole the suit some time ago, and then a few days later he killed himself. I believe he stole it to see his wife in the next world — your world. But she's dead here too. The disappointment must have killed him. But here you are. So my spider-sense is telling me that she is alive in the world after this one. Am I right?"

Mark nodded.

"It's OK for you to speak, you know," prompted Brad.

Mark coughed into his hand and then examined it. More blood. He glanced back at the splatter on the floor.

"OK, fine, I'll talk. But walk with me. I have to clean things up here. What are you doing in here, anyway? I mean, I take it that you're the one that's been playing jokes on us. You got the Brad here in deep trouble by doing that, by the way. In any case, I do appreciate that you didn't punk me..."

"Well, I'd thought that you were dead," interjected Brad.

"...but what I'm getting at, is why the hell are you in this room? Aren't you afraid of the cameras?"

Brad waved his free hand dismissively and said, "Ah, well, naturally I have them rigged back home. But true, usually I avoid this room. But, you know, I just finished messing around and was standing out in the hallway about to flick back over and walk through the door in my own world when something in the back of my brain said, "Let's just have a peek.""

"That was needlessly risky, wasn't it?" suggested Mark.

"Yeah, well," explained Brad while gesturing at the suit he was wearing, "I'm not exactly adverse to risk, am I?" As an afterthought he added, "Between you and me bro... the salt and the sugar... are switched." He crossed his arms in demonstration.

Mark nodded as he scrubbed the blood off the floor. Then he replied, "Thanks, bro. I'll tell you something good too, then. After tomorrow, this place is getting shut down for at least a week while they drastically up security. Unfortunately for both of us, I have no idea what that entails. But I'd say, thrill seeker or not, you better be careful."

"Dude, thanks," replied Brad. "We're actually doing the same thing. Some complete bastard has been sneaking in and messing around with everything." He shook his head in mock disdain.

Mark stood up, glanced at his watch, and said, "Well, not that it hasn't been tremendous fun, but I really have to be getting the hell out of here. And I imagine so do you. If you ever manage to figure out the security system, be sure to pop in for a cup of tea or something, OK?"

"Yeah, you got it, bro," replied Brad. He watched Mark as he stuffed the bloody gauze into a plastic bag and added, "And you get that cough looked at, OK? Although, we both know it isn't going to get any better if you keep walking through these walls. You might want to reflect on that. And also think about what it's doing to the rest of your body."

Mark stared at the bloody gauze and said nothing.

Brad moved his hand to his arm and was about to flick back to his own world when Mark suddenly called out, "Wait!"

Brad waited.

Mark asked, "So wait, how are you getting outside with the suit, then?"

Brad smiled and said, "Well, I've only left a couple of times, but I generally use the front door."

"How?" asked Mark.

"Charm," replied Brad while hiking up his smile another notch.

"Unlikely," replied Mark.

Brad laughed. "No, really, the guard at the door is cool as hell. You ever talk to him?"

"Samuel? The old guy who gibbers philosophy? Yes, I've talked to him but I'm always too tired to fully engage him."

Brad raised his hand to his arm again and replied, "Maybe you should reflect on that too, my friend."

"Yeah, right. I'll do that," replied Mark.

Brad gave him a nod. "Later, bro."

"Later," replied Mark with a returning nod.

Brad flipped a switch and was gone.

Mark stared at the empty air and said, "This has been a very odd day. I can't imagine many other people have had days as weird as this one."

He then set about returning the suit to its stand and performing his ritual of hiding his tracks.

After he was finished with the room, he cautiously left it. He was as tired and confused as ever. Different snippets of conversation from the night kept playing back in his mind, some with Lisa and some with Brad. Suddenly he stopped walking and mumbled to himself, "Wait, what? He knew that I stole the suit? I wonder if the Brad here knows too? Hmm. Better I don't ask."

Mark resumed walking.

At the front door, a deep, friendly voice said, "Ah, Mr. Scottsdale. All done for the night? I know it's not my place to say such things, but you look like a two day old dog turd. Maybe you're working a little too hard. Life is all about balance, is it not?"

Mark laughed at the sudden informality. "It's Samuel, right?"

"Yes, but my friends call me Samuel."

Mark blinked. "OK... Samuel."

"Can I give you some advice?" asked Samuel, suddenly.

Mark considered this and said, "Uh, yeah, sure. I don't know if I'm awake enough to understand it, though."

"Don't worry. It's real simple," said Samuel, reassuringly.

"OK," replied Mark with a lazy half shrug.

Samuel looked left and right, then with a lowered voice he said, "Stop all this foolishness before it gets you killed."

Mark's brain formed several replies in rapid succession and then tried to give all of them to his mouth at once. One was titled "Deny," another was "Play Stupid," a third read "Truth." The last one was titled "WTF?" Mark's mouth picked one at random — it was "Truth." Then his mouth, being much more savvy than his currently overtaxed brain, read what it was supposed to say, rejected it, and forwarded the message to Mark's neck in the form of a simple command.

Mark nodded humbly.

Samuel gave him a fatherly smile and then said, "Good, that's settled then. You get yourself some sleep now, Mr.

Scottsdale."

Mark nodded again as he walked past the guard. He waved one hand lazily as he did so and said, "Mark. Call me Mark."

CHAPTER 36

———————— ▼ ————————

As the theme song to *Mission Impossible* played on continuous loop inside Mark's head, he and Pryb stealthily worked their way to the front entrance of the building.

Occasionally Pryb would sharply raise a hand and the two would instantly stop together. It would have been clear to an outside observer (had there been any outside observers, but of course the whole point of this endeavor was to not have been seen by any such outside observers) that Pryb must have spent the last couple of weeks teaching Mark the basics of his craft, and we are not talking about the craft of cabinet installation or bathroom tiling.

Pryb raise his hand and they both stopped again. He scanned the area with his infrared binoculars. Then, as he sighted along something that looked like a flashlight mounted on a tiny tripod, he explained to Mark, "It looks like they are using infrared cameras. Now see, if they were smart they'd simply use super low light cameras because infrared cameras still cannot see in the dark. Not really. They need to use an infrared light source to light up the scene. Humans can't see the light, but the cameras can. And so can these binoculars. So what I'm doing here, is setting up these infrared lights to shine right back at the cameras. The cameras don't like that — it's like staring at the sun to them."

"Won't someone notice?" asked Mark, quite rationally.

Pryb rubbed his chin and said, "Probably new guards... likely to be very keen on their first week... Yep. Almost certainly."

"Then why are we doing it?" asked Mark with a hint of worry in his voice.

Pryb glared at him and said, "Because, when I told someone we should wait awhile before breaking in, he was all like, 'Oh, but I'll just die if I don't see my beloved Lisa right away.'" He wrapped his arms around himself in a parody of a couple embracing.

Mark frowned.

"We'll figure something out," reassured Pryb. "Come on, let's just go."

The two crept along the side of the building and approached the front door. Pryb said that most security is usually concentrated in the back of a building because no one thinks anyone would be stupid enough to go in through the front door.

Mark mumbled, "Obviously they never met us."

Pryb ignored this and directed Mark to insert a specially prepared card into a slot on the door. Mark did this and Pryb immediately ran through the opening door and immobilized the guard.

Mark cautiously followed him inside and saw the guard lying on the floor, not moving but still breathing.

Mark hissed, "Dude! What did you do to Samuel? He's cool. He would have helped us."

Pryb dropped his tool bag noisily on the ground and turned sharply to Mark. Agitated, he held his arms away from his body and said, "What do you mean, he's cool and would have helped us? He's cool? He's cool! Do you think sometime in the last few weeks while we were meticulously planning and training you could have, oh, I don't know, sort of mentioned that you were tight with the front door guard? Didn't you think that maybe, just maybe, that might have been, oh, I don't know, a little helpful for me to know?"

Samuel slowly sat up and rubbed the back of his head.

Mark replied, "Well I'm sorry. I've had a lot of things on my mind, haven't I? And besides, I wasn't totally sure he would help us. Honestly, I figured we would be doing some kind of Mission-Impossible-dropping-through-the-skylights-and-crawling-through-the-ductwork sort of thing."

Samuel mumbled to himself, "I probably would have helped if it meant not getting hit on the head with a wrench."

"What?!? There are skylights here? When were you planning on telling me this?" exploded Pryb. "I mean, is there anything else you'd like to share? The existence of a hidden tunnel, perhaps?"

Samuel was to his feet now and watching the two fight with a mixture of amusement and disappointment. It took a few seconds before they noticed him. When they finally did notice, he said, "Look, Mark, are you sure you want to go through with this?"

Mark felt Pryb tense up next to him and held a restraining hand in front of him. He then answered, "I'm not entirely sure that you know what 'this' is, and I'm not — contrary to what my friend here might say — stupid enough to reveal it, but yes, the only thing I'm sure about in this world right now is that I need to do 'this.'"

Samuel reached into his pocket. Pryb tensed. Mark tensed. Samuel pulled out a key. Everyone relaxed.

He pointed to a door a few feet away and said, "That's the main electrical closet. The labs need a lot of electricity. Most of the cabling is under the floor. There's an access panel in the floor. They didn't bother to secure it. You can drop down in there and it will take you right to Plan A's lab. I'll disable the security from here. You grab the suit and come back out this way."

Samuel noticed the looks on their faces and asked, "Is there a problem?"

Mark started to answer but Pryb interrupted. He raised his hands over his head and said in exasperation, "Oh my god, there really was a secret tunnel. I give up. I quit. I'm going home."

Mark ignored him and replied to Samuel, "So you really do know what I'm after, then. How?"

Samuel replied, "Me and Brad play cards on Thursday nights, and we talk about this and that." His normally placid expression seemed to waver for the merest of seconds and then he asked, "Look, Mark, are you sure you won't quit this foolishness and go home?"

Mark shook his head. "Thank you for worrying about me, but my mind is made up."

"I'm sorry to hear that," replied Samuel. "Here's your key."

"Thanks," replied Mark. "I owe you one." He and Pryb turned to go.

Samuel said to their backs, "You owe me about a million, Mark, but you can start paying me back by not getting caught. I'll be in real trouble if you get caught, and I'm not talking about a paid suspension. These people can get downright medieval when it comes to national security. I'm serious here, man. Don't get caught."

Pryb turned around briefly and said, "Don't worry, mister,

I'm a professional at this stuff. No worries." He then grabbed Mark by the back of the collar, pulled him backwards, and then gently nudged him in front of a different door while muttering, "Wrong door, you idiot." He glanced back at the guard and flicked him a reassuring smile.

A few minutes later, as they were walking through the access tunnels, Pryb said cheerily, "See, I told you we'd figure something out."

CHAPTER 37

▼

Lisa heard her doorbell ring. She opened the door to find a man wearing silver spandex and an astronaut's helmet. He had a dozen roses in his hand. Her mouth opened but she said nothing.

The would-be astronaut said, "I hope you like these. They're, uh, from your neighbor's yard, actually. I can't exactly go into a florist looking like this and besides, I have no money because, well," he glanced down, "no pockets."

Lisa's mouth shut. Lisa's mouth opened again. Words came out. The words were, "Blobby Bob?"

"Mark. The name is Mark, remember? But yes, it's me. I've got a cool new suit now. What do you think?" He spun around.

Lisa answered, "I think you better get inside before the neighbors think I'm receiving a strip-o-gram or something." She grabbed his hand and tugged him inside.

After some thought, she tugged him back outside into the back yard where they settled into some comfortable patio furniture.

Mark looked around at the yard. It was surrounded by tall bushes — very private. He glanced at the garden and said, "It looks like you've kept up on the garden. Very nice."

Lisa smiled and said, "Yes, well, it reminds me of you now so I've spent a lot of time out here." She blushed.

Inside his helmet, Mark raised an eyebrow. Lisa examined the helmet and said, "Feel free to remove your helmet and make yourself comfortable."

Mark shook his head slightly and said, "I'd love to, but from what I know, if any part of me is outside the suit while I'm here, it instantly gets projected back into my own world — in little tiny pieces."

"I'd keep the helmet on, then," suggested Lisa.

"Yes, good idea," replied Mark.

There was a moment of silence while each sought for another topic of conversation. Lisa eventually broke it by saying, "So, I did some digging around and I couldn't find any record of you at all."

"Really?" asked Mark in disbelief.

"Really," replied Lisa. "Not a single Blobby Bob anywhere in any records."

"It's Mark," replied Mark, automatically. They both smiled.

Lisa continued, "Seriously though, I did actually do some proper research and I couldn't find any record of your birth."

"Really?" repeated Mark.

"Really," repeated Lisa. "There's more to it, though. Your parents here still married each other, and your mom did get pregnant, but in this world it seems that you were stillborn — strangled by the umbilical cord, apparently. So it looks like you won't have to fight yourself for my affection after all. That's good, right?" She smiled and added, "Although now that you tell me that nothing can leave your suit, I'm a little worried about the logistics of a full-fledged relationship."

It was now Mark's turn to blush.

CHAPTER 38

▼

"You look awfully cheerful today," said Tammy as she sat down across from Mark at the cafeteria table. He was humming to himself as he ate.

He looked up at her and said, "My dear Tammy. Here — have a pudding cup." He slid his chocolate pudding over to her side of the table.

Tammy smiled and said, "Thanks. It's rare to see you in such a good mood. Normally you look sulky and preoccupied. Did something good happen? Don't tell me... you got a girlfriend, is that it?"

Mark swallowed and said, "Yeah, no, not really. I mean, yes, things are finally looking up for me, but sadly, no, I wouldn't say I had a new girlfriend. Not really."

Tammy, as perceptive as always, said, "Ah, but you're hoping you will soon."

Mark nodded. "Yes... you could say that."

"Anyone I know?" asked Tammy.

"I doubt it," replied Mark. "You two are worlds apart."

For some reason that Tammy could not fathom, this made Mark laugh to himself.

Tammy wrinkled her forehead at him, although this was not visible under her hair. She pushed some of it away from her eyes and said, "Yes, well, I'm right here and I won't lead you on like this girl. You're just going to end up with a broken heart; I can tell. How about you just forget about her and go out with me instead?"

Tammy always pictured Mark as a sort of gangly baby lamb. It was therefore that much more surprising when he metaphorically turned around and bit her arm off.

Mark said, "You're only interested in me because I turned

you down. Men don't normally turn you down, do they? It makes you want to break me. In reality, though, you don't really know anything about me. What if the walls of my house were lined with little porcelain dolls and I liked to wear my mom's slippers and owned a shaved cat that I called Harry?"

Tammy blinked at Mark's odd barrage of penetrating insight, creepy sarcasm, and off-color humor.

Mark went back to eating.

After a moment, Tammy said, "You should just give up now and do what I say. You'll be much happier if you do, or, to put it another way, you'll be much sadder if you don't."

"Are you seriously threatening me?" asked Mark, his voice suddenly like ice. "There might have been a chance that I'd date you at one time, but now I just want you out of my sight. That's plain creepy. What kind of psycho threatens people into going out with them? I mean, really."

Tammy, embarrassed and insulted, stood up and left the cafeteria without a word. Mark shivered.

CHAPTER 39

———————▼———————

Lisa was humming to herself as she loaded the centrifuge with another set of samples. Sharon noticed this as she walked into the lab. She walked over to Lisa and gave her side a pinch.

Lisa said, "Ah!" and playfully brushed Sharon's hand away.

Sharon said, "Sorry. You just looked so cute standing there humming to yourself that I had to pinch you. So, I take it things are going well with you and Blobby Bob. Are you two getting married soon? Is the wedding going to be held on the moon? And what about the honeymoon? Do you think he can alter the suit, you know, down below?"

Lisa blushed and stared fixedly at the centrifuge. She exhaled and said, "His name is Mark. And yes, things are going really well between us. He visits twice a week now. He's really quite brave. He told me what he has to do to get the suit. He's basically committing a felony by stealing top secret government equipment just to date me."

Sharon smiled and said, "So what you are saying is that someone would definitely notice if he sewed a tube onto the front of the suit. That's a pity."

Lisa blushed again and said, "We'll figure something out. I'll talk to him tonight. Maybe there is some way for him to come here without the suit."

"I hope so," replied Sharon. "Then maybe you can return to the night shift on Tuesdays and Thursdays like the old days. It's lonely here without you." She thought for a moment and added, "So anyway, when am I going to get to meet this Blobby Mark of yours? It's not that I don't believe you or anything, but you really have my curiosity up and I'd like to give my approval before you go and run off with a spaceman from another dimension."

"We will see," replied Lisa. "He's very reluctant about that sort of thing. I think he worries about disrupting the intended timeline of our dimension, or something along those lines. I told him that he's already altered my life and distracted me from my work — work which could have potentially produced life-changing results but might now never materialize thanks to him. It doesn't seem to change his mind."

"Well it wouldn't, would it?" argued Sharon.

"Perhaps when he is here permanently," offered Lisa with hope in her voice, "then I'll introduce you to him. I think you two would really enjoy being sarcastic to each other."

CHAPTER 40

─────────▼─────────

"It's a pity that you can't visit during the day, Mark," said Lisa while holding his hand on the couch. They were watching the meerkat show together.

Mark turned his helmeted head toward Lisa and frowned. "I know. And it's frustrating having to wear this suit too. Apart from the obvious inconvenience of not being able to actually touch you, or kiss you, it's also not the most subtle of things to wear out in public. I worry that it's getting boring for you."

Lisa turned to face him on the couch and held his hand between both of hers. "I was worried about the same thing — that you might get bored and leave. I never will. If this is all we can do, then I accept that."

Mark hugged her while a small tear of relief formed under his eye. His visor started to fog, causing him to have to turn up the suit's air conditioning temporarily. He jokingly said, "OK, now don't go and make me cry, you know my visor fogs up and then I have to waste battery power to defog it." He released the hug.

Lisa smiled and said, "Still, it would be nice, though, wouldn't it? For us to be together like a normal couple? Do you think the people at your work will ever get the technology to that point?"

Mark nodded optimistically. "I'm sure of it. After all, the project has the government's backing. And what do all governments want to do?"

"Rape and pillage?" suggested Lisa.

"Graphic," admitted Mark, "but accurate. I'm pretty sure that their ultimate goal is to try to take the natural resources from this world and bring them back to ours. So it follows that they will have to figure out a way for things to travel between the two without the aid of a suit or some sort of encapsulation."

Lisa frowned. "I'm not sure if I should be happy or sad about that. I mean, yes, that's great that you might be able to come here for real, but I have to admit that I'm not too keen on your world basically declaring war on mine. After all, that's what we are talking about here, isn't it?"

Mark frowned. "I wasn't thinking about it quite like that. I sort of pictured them quietly stealing resources in the dead of night."

"Yes, but Mark, eventually someone is going to notice. Things will get ugly."

Mark frowned again. "Damn. You're right. Well, I'll think of something. Maybe once they get the tech, I can use it to come here, and maybe sabotage the project when I do. I'm sure Pryb can figure something out."

Lisa shook her head. "I still can't believe that my dorky accountant is a criminal mastermind in your world. It just doesn't fit."

Mark grinned. "Apparently, that's all down to my influence in his life."

Lisa said enticingly, "Really? Wow. You don't say. Then how about you come a little closer and see if you can corrupt me as well?" She removed one of her hands from his hand and placed it somewhere else.

Mark's visor fogged again.

CHAPTER 41

---▼---

Mark sat down on the edge of his bed and began reading the latest entry in the test pilot's journal. Pryb stopped using the computer and turned to listen.

Good day to you nerds and nerdettes! I've got some amazing news today — I just saved 10% on my car insurance! OK, no, seriously, I do have some cool things to share. Although, as I've said a thousand times before, I don't know why I have to write this stuff down since everyone already knows it, and probably knows it better than me, but I digress...

Firstly, some interesting news from the philosophy-of-life front. It seems that some recent evidence suggests that the next world is sometimes torn down and subtly rewritten in between clock cycles of this world. As yet, there is no way of knowing how much "time" this takes since time appears to be a swimmy and unreliable entity in this current world view. Relative to us, however, it is almost instantaneous. At least that's the current line of thought.

What's more, the white coats believe that this rewriting is happening as a result of choices made in this world. I know, I know.

You are calling B.S. here, right? But I've seen it myself. I've been in town in the new suit. I've watched a woman get hit by a car here, only to flip into the other world to see that she had decided not to cross the street at the last moment.

Against the rules, I approached her and asked her why she had hesitated. Here is what she said: "What are you? Some kind of astronaut?"

But after I had explained that I was just an eccentric and out of work actor, she relaxed and explained herself to me by saying this: "I don't know... I just sort of had a really bad feeling so I didn't. Now leave me alone. I'm late for work."

Remarkable. The white coats were so happy by this discovery that they did not beat me with chains like the last time I had broken the rules. Could we have just discovered the source of déjà vu? Have we just shown that reincarnation does, in a sense, actually occur, and that we get a chance in another life to correct our mistakes? Or, as some of the grumpier white coats have put it, is this all nothing but hogwash and circumstance? Either way, exciting times are ahead.

And speaking of exciting times, the applied science team feels they are very close to being able to hack things into and out of the next world without a suit. We're talking full, unfettered, inter-dimensional interaction here! Way cool. I have to admit, I will miss the feeling of spandex on my body. Perhaps one day I will quit this job and join the Blue Man Group.

Mark put down the paper. Pryb looked at him and asked flatly, "You're going to move there, aren't you?"

"It just makes sense," Mark replied. "She doesn't have a Mark, and I don't have a Lisa."

"And you're just going to leave your life-long buddy here to fend for himself, are you?" asked Pryb. He was smiling, but Mark knew there was genuine sadness behind it.

Mark considered this. "Come with me," he suggested. "Think about it. There is a whole world out there that's never seen a Pryb that isn't a sad, little accountant. A world that might need your unique services. And when you think about it, some of your targets would be pushovers since you've probably already encountered them before."

"Oh, I don't know," Pryb began. "I mean, I'm sure that world has plenty of other guys who can install marble counter tops and vinyl flooring."

Mark laughed. "Yes, but none that can do it with your sense of style, I'm sure."

Pryb drummed his fingers on the chair's armrest for a moment and then said, "Oh, the hell with it. Count me in. You only live once, eh?"

CHAPTER 42

———————▼———————

"Oh, Mark, I see you brought your friend with you tonight," said Samuel while folding his paper and setting it on the guard station's desk. He noticed the suitcases and added, "Are you planning to stay a while?"

"You might say that," replied Mark. He set down his suit cases and shook the guard's hand. "I just wanted to say thanks. Really, thank you. I can't tell you how much you've helped me, and how happy I am now, thanks to you." He let go of Samuel's hand and added, "This will be the last night that I'll bother you. You won't see either of us after tonight. So... uh, once again, thank you. And also, goodbye."

Samuel studied Mark's face for a good while and then said, "Well, far be it from me to interfere in another man's happiness. I don't know what you two are planning, but just do old Samuel here a favor and don't leave a mess. I wasn't born to have my fingers smashed one-by-one by an irate employer."

Mark made a face at Samuel. "Now, come on, you don't think Steve would do something like that, do you?"

It was now Samuel's turn to make a face. "You've known him longer than me. What do you think?"

Mark thought about the not so subtle aroma of the mafia that always seemed to flow around his employer. He said, "Point taken. I'll be careful."

Mark and Pryb then tried to open the electrical closet but the key was not working. Samuel came up behind them and said, "Oh, right. Sorry about that, but that route is now secure. You'll have to walk through the hall. I'll handle things from here, as always, but you better be careful of the other guards. They don't follow a set routine, so it's going to be tough. Actually, I'll tell you what, just this once I'll set up a little diversion for you —

draw them to the other side of the building."

"Dude, Samuel, thanks again so much," Mark opined.

Samuel nodded, and the two picked up their suitcases and began the walk to the back of building. As promised, Samuel called the guards on the radio and asked them to check something out on the opposite wing of the building.

"You know," began Pryb while studying the interior of the building out of professional habit, "I'm not really seeing what all the fuss was about. I mean, the security here is frankly a joke. Even without the guard's help, I bet you and me could have strolled right through here as bold as we liked. Now me, I'd have, like, lasers and stuff right here, and at least some sort of thermal detection system. I mean, really. Who relies on lazy, old guards to secure probably the most secretive project on the planet? It makes me want to weep. I bet even my old grandma could..."

<SLAM!>

Pryb's words were cut off by a thunderous, metallic clang that echoed several times up and down the corridor until finally fading away, leaving only a ringing in Mark's ears. About 50 feet in front of them, a steel wall had dropped down from the ceiling and blocked their path. Mark was going to turn around and say something sarcastic like, "You were saying?" but he had heard the loud noise right behind him as well and was now getting a sick feeling in his stomach.

He slowly turned around. His friend had been crushed underneath the second steel wall. Blood was oozing from his bifurcated mid section. Pryb briefly looked at Mark, gurgled, and died. Blood flowed from his mouth and mingled with the blood from his gut.

Mark crumbled. There was no dramatic shouting of "No!!!" like in the movies, and no hugging of the corpse, just the full mental shutdown of a man in shock. He went completely limp and lay motionless on the floor while watching his friend's blood move towards his face like a rolling wave. He passed out.

CHAPTER 43

---▼---

Mark woke up to pain. His ribs ached, as did his head.

He opened his eyes to a dull gray ceiling. Turning his head to the side gave him a nice view of a dull gray wall. In the center of the wall were sturdy looking iron bars. This, he decided, was not good.

He sat up and looked around again. The view did not improve, nor did his prospects of a happy, carefree life. A red light on top of a camera blinked at him from just outside his cell.

He heard footsteps echoing from someplace down an unseen hallway. They were getting louder. After a while, a man appeared. It was Steve.

Steve made sure that Mark had his full attention. Then he began to blast Mark with verbal abuse.

"I can't believe you did this to me, Mark. I thought we were pals. Here I am, being a nice guy, helping an old friend out with a new start in life, and he stabs me in the back. You stole from me, and you made me look like a fool to the green shirts. Do you know they are thinking of taking the whole project from me now thanks to you?"

"I..." began Mark.

"You can just shut the hell up, is what you can do. Jesus. You must think I'm stupid. You must think I'm unfit even to write my own name. Did you really think that all this time you were fooling me? You really thought a top secret facility had such a cheap system in place? You really thought that seeing my secretary logging into the system at odd hours and changing alarm settings wasn't going to raise some red flags?"

"I just..." began Mark again.

"Shut up. Now tell me, why did you do it, Mark? Money? Did I not pay you enough? Who were you going to give the suit to? We saw your hideout in that abandoned building. Is it the Russians? The Iranians? Well? Answer me."

"I just used it to see a girl," answered Mark.

Steve's face turned red. He put his hand on one panel while typing a code into another. He opened the door, walked in, closed the door behind him, and then began to hit Mark repeatedly in the face while yelling, "I almost felt bad for kicking you last night while you were passed out, but now I'm going to beat that smart ass attitude out of you but good, and I won't lose any sleep over it tonight, I assure you."

Mark passed out.

Time passed.

Mark woke up to pain. His ribs ached, as did his head. And now so did his face.

He opened his eyes to a dull gray ceiling. Turning his head to the side gave him a nice view of a dull gray wall. In the center of the wall were sturdy looking iron bars. This, he decided, was still not good.

He sat up. A ball of reddish-blonde hair was staring at him from outside his cell. The hair said, "I told you that you should have gone out with me, Mark."

"Tammy?" Mark asked, just to be sure.

Tammy shook her hair to one side and said, "Of course it's me, you dope. You look like crap, by the way."

"You... You turned me in, didn't you?"

"Yeah, I did," replied Tammy, "but Steve already knew. They noticed the weird log-ins by Doreen and utilized my research to monitor everyone. Steve wasn't going to have us bug you at first, but then Samuel tipped him off. Steve really trusted you. I can't tell you how mad he was when he found out."

"You don't have to," said Mark. "Just look at my face."

"I'd rather not. It's pretty hideous right now," Tammy replied.

"I can imagine," said Mark with a sigh. "So, Samuel turned me in too? Damn. But you know, in a weird way that makes me feel better. I mean, it appears I would have been caught one way or another, so I'm glad he's not going down with me."

"You know, Mark, I'm glad to hear you say that," said Samuel while stepping into view. "It is my job to keep this place secure, after all. I mean, they don't hire the sort of person who's going to say, 'Hey, you seem like a nice guy, go ahead and walk out with that top secret prototype,' to guard this type of place, do they? And to be fair, I did ask you nicely to quit all of your foolishness. Three times, if I remember correctly."

Mark said meekly, "Yeah. No, I understand." He patted his face gingerly with his hand to try to survey the damage, and then said, "So, what happens now?"

"Now," said Samuel smoothly, "they beat you once a day until you tell them why you stole the suit."

"But I already told Steve why I did it — to see my wife. Well, my wife in the next world."

"And what did he say?" asked Samuel.

"He gave me this," replied Mark, pointing at his face.

"Looks like he didn't believe you."

Mark snorted. "No. No he did not."

"Well, good luck with that. I have to go now. They don't really like it when us guards get too chatty with the inmates."

Samuel and Tammy both turned to go. Mark called out, "By the way, where am I?"

Samuel stopped walking for a moment and said, "Mmmm, as far as you're concerned, hell," and then he walked away.

Tammy made a rude gesture and then followed him.

CHAPTER 44

—————▼—————

Days passed. Days passed slowly. Days passed slowly and painfully.

Mark had lost Lisa forever now — both of them — along with his best friend. He had lost his freedom, he was losing his mind, and he had definitely lost his will to live.

No matter how many times that Mark had pleaded with him, Steve would not believe him when he said that he had stolen the suit simply to visit his dead wife. In the end, Mark had tried to make up a story about Russians in the hopes that it would be believed and the beatings would end, but since he had no solid details to back up his assertion, Steve hadn't believed that story either and the beatings continued.

It was now clear to Mark that there would be no trial, no appeal, and no mercy. The beatings would continue forever.

It might have been two months now, perhaps more. Mark had no way to note the passage of time other than his own erratic sleep cycle. His body was in tatters, and so was his soul. The only thing he wanted out of life now was for it to end. He had reached his limit. He could bear no more suffering.

As strange as it sounds, jails are built expressly to make it difficult for an inmate to kill himself. There was certainly very little in Mark's cell that he could use toward this end. He did have a sheet, but there was nothing to hang it from.

His bed frame had been bolted to the wall and the frame itself had thick steel sheets welded onto it specifically to prevent him from doing what he was trying to do.

Mark inspected the welds. They were definitely sub-par on one of the panels. Obviously this place had been built by the lowest bidder, he decided.

He now had a plan, and it would work. With this realization, a Zen-like calm came over him.

He stood up and stretched. It hurt to do so. He folded his bed sheet across two opposite corners and twisted it into a tight rope. He then sat down on the floor and began to kick seven kinds of hell out of the one panel until several welds broke loose and it bent inward slightly.

Mark quickly shoved the fabricated rope through the new opening and around the frame, and then tied the two loose ends together.

Suddenly alarms rang into life all throughout the facility. Mark saw a fire warning light flashing outside his cell. Well, he thought, it's not really any concern of mine at this point.

There were rushed footsteps in the distance now. He had to hurry. While sitting with his back to the bed, he put the rope around his neck, held it in place with both hands, laid back, and began to spin.

All he had to do to be free from all this pain was to spin. He spun, and spun, and spun. Before the rushing feet could make it to him, the rope tightened around Mark's neck and he breathed his final breath.

Steve stood outside of Mark's cell and cursed. "God damn it! All the data is gone and there is fire everywhere. Who the hell was he working with?"

Tammy replied, "It's possible that either he or his dead friend might have had some sort of 'in case of death' system in place. You know, the sort of thing you have to access every few days, and if you don't then all hell breaks loose."

"We didn't check for that?" Steve snapped.

"We did, but they were pretty clever. There is another possibility, though."

"What?"

Tammy flicked the hair away from one eye and said, "Brad, the test pilot, didn't come to work today."

A large boom shook the entire building. Concrete dust rained down on them. Steve said, "Let's go."

Before Tammy could answer, several thousand tons of molten metal and concrete poured over them and hissed as they were both vaporized. Soon, the entire place filled with fiery, liquid death.

CHAPTER 45

By the end of the first month after Mark had suddenly stopped visiting her, Lisa had begun to really worry about him. She had also been surprised at just how much she had missed him. During the next month, it was hard for her to think about anything else. As a result of this, both her work and her health began to suffer. Near the end of the third month, she took a leave of absence from her job in order to search for clues in finding him again.

She started her search by finding the abandoned high school that Mark had claimed was the location of the laboratory in his world. She spent a week camping inside the school in the hopes that she would catch either Mark or one of his coworkers during a visit, but all she caught was a cold from sleeping on the concrete floor.

The next thing she tried was to hunt down the owner of the facility, Steve Bastille. Unfortunately, when she finally found him, he turned out to be the owner of several used car lots across much of Southern California, and he claimed to know nothing about any such research facility or the Flicker project.

During this period, Lisa's coworker, Sharon, had stopped by to visit Lisa a few times to plead with her to let go of her obsession and come back to work. Unfortunately, Lisa had a manic drive about her and could not focus on anything else. Sharon eventually gave up trying to convince her but did continue to visit once a week just to make sure that Lisa was eating properly.

Lisa was now at a loss as to what to do next. As a last ditch effort, she began to research the Simulation Hypothesis. She even went as far as tracking down some of its biggest proponents in the hopes of putting together some kind of team. Unfortunately for her, she lacked the charisma and financial backing needed to get such an ambitious project off the ground.

Now, after several months without any contact from Mark, she knew in her heart that she would never see him again. Up until this point she was not letting herself believe it, but the truth was finally sinking in and it was devastating for her. She had finally met the missing person in her life, the one that complemented her perfectly, and just like that he was utterly lost to her.

Pausing only to write an apology letter to Sharon, Lisa went to her medicine cabinet, selected five random drugs, and took them all. Mercifully, on this one occasion, she got the mixture and proportions exactly right and had a painless death while in a drug-induced sleep.

CHAPTER 46

In World(+1), Mark was conceived in the back of a Volkswagen Microbus. All indications were that he was to be a healthy baby boy. However, just before his birth, a remnant of a previous life entered his mind. The remnant was an action wrapped in strong emotion, and it commanded Mark to spin and spin and spin. And so he did. As a result of this, Mark tragically died before he could be born.

CHAPTER 47

———————— ▼ ————————

In World(+2), Mr. and Mrs. Brabham became the proud parents of a healthy baby girl in a sleepy town in Michigan. Her mother called her Lisa after the oldest daughter on the *Simpsons*.

A month and a half later, and also in World(+2), Mr. and Mrs. Scottsdale became the proud parents of a healthy baby boy in a bustling town in California. His mother named him Mark after the thankfully temporary mark on his forehead from the time when the nurse had inadvertently banged him on the side railings of the hospital bed while endeavoring to pass him to her.

Mark grew up to be a fairly normal child. When he was five, he nearly burnt the house down when he discovered the magic door at the bottom of the dryer. After the smoke had cleared, his parents explained to him that it was a door to access the pilot light, and he wasn't to go near it again.

When Mark was in first grade, he learned the rudiments of critical thinking and the scientific method from his beloved science teacher, Mr. Parker. By second grade, he realized that religion made no sense to him in that it sounded more like fairy tales for adults rather than anything that would really happen. Unfortunately, most adults got angry with him when he told them this, especially during Sunday School.

About a month and a half before Mark's tenth Birthday, a new family moved into the house next door to his. While doing homework at his desk, Mark saw the moving truck through his bedroom window as it pulled into the driveway next door. He paid no more attention to it until he happened to see a mother, a father, and a little girl walking up his driveway. The little girl had caught his eye, with her bright red dress and her long, wavy blonde curls.

A short time later, the doorbell rang. Mark raced downstairs wearing a pair of cut-off jeans and a Spider Man T-shirt. He nearly opened the door himself but remembered his father's stern warnings just in time and waited patiently for his parents to come to the door first. He then anxiously opened the door with his father's permission.

Mark peered out of the door. There were two adults standing there, but Mark barely noticed them. His full attention was on the little girl with the long, blonde curls. Most of her body was hidden behind her father, but Mark could see her piercing green eyes looking back at him from his shadow.

The adults started talking, but Mark was not listening to what they had to say. He and the little girl continued to stare wordlessly at each other until he was eventually nudged by his mother, who then said, "Mark! Answer your father."

Mark felt like he had just been woken up from some kind of dream. He looked quickly from his mother to his father. His father laughed the laugh of an adult who in other circumstances would have given Mark a quick smack to the back of the head. He then said, "Mark, I said, why don't you and Lisa here go play outside together until dinner is ready?"

Mark looked at Lisa again. She hid further behind her father but continued to stare at Mark with one emerald eye.

Mark said to her, "I know where some frogs live out back. You want to go see?"

Lisa shyly nodded and partially unhid herself from behind her father's legs.

Mark said, "Cool. Come on." He then grasped her lightly by the hand and gently led her around the house and into the back yard. Lisa, who was normally shy even around her own teddy bear, felt instantly at ease with Mark and followed him without hesitation.

Lisa's eyes went wide when she saw that there was a large natural pond in the back of the property. It was partially in the shade of a few tall trees that looked like they were being slowly strangled by vines. It looked like a tiny piece of paradise to her. She was amazed that anyone would have such a thing in their back yard. Her own yard in her previous home had merely been a patch of grass surrounded by a rusty chain link fence.

At the front of the house, the adults smiled as they watched little Mark and Lisa disappear around the side of the house. Lisa's mother said, "Oh, my little girl found herself a little playmate. Isn't that great? Oh my." She reached into her sleeve and produced a wadded up tissue, which she then used to dab at her eyes in an effort to dry them.

Seeing this, Lisa's father said, "I'm sorry; my wife is a very emotional person. Now, now — that's enough dear."

Mark's mother said, "Oh, don't be silly. It's fine."

And his father added, "Yes, fine. Nothing to be ashamed of. Please, come on in and relax while we prepare dinner. You two must be exhausted from your drive."

Lisa's mother replied, "Oh my gosh. Thank you. I'm so glad we moved into this neighborhood. You two are such nice people."

The adults then went inside and made typical adult small talk. Meanwhile, out back in the pond, Lisa was drowning.

Mark had just shown her how he could sneak up and grab a frog from behind to catch it. Lisa, intrigued, had just tried to replicate his technique only to slip on the muddy bank and fall into the pond.

Mark watched in horror as she flailed around wildly and sank under the water. It was plain to Mark that she either could not swim or was too panicked to do so. He attempted to grab her hand from the bank, but that only resulted in him sliding into the pond as well.

Mark knew how to doggy paddle, but he was in no way a strong enough swimmer to stay above water and hold her in any useful way at the same time. He knew that the pond was usually just above head height, so in desperation he dove under her, grabbed her legs, and pushed off the bottom of the pond using all the strength his legs could deliver.

This propelled Lisa upward enough that she was able to grab a few of the vines that were wrapped around a tree on the edge of the pond and use them to scrabble to shore. Mark, on the other hand, now had both of his feet stuck in the muddy pond bottom while his head was about six inches under water.

Lisa could see the panic on Mark's face while he struggled to free himself. She knew the vines were strong, so she tugged on them until there was enough slack to reach Mark. She then tossed the slack vine loops to Mark, whose flailing hands eventually found one. He tugged on the vine with all of his strength, which was mercifully just enough to free him. His shoes, however, were never seen again.

Children often don't have the emotional maturity nor the vocabulary to see them through times like this. This was certainly the case with Mark and Lisa. However, they did each know exactly what had just happened, which was that, in a very real sense, they had just saved each other's lives.

So, being emotionally immature and filled to the brim with the relief of being alive and the happiness of a newly formed bond, they did what felt natural to them at the time, which was to laugh and laugh and laugh until tears ran down their cheeks.

After the shock had finally worn off, they did something else that comes naturally to children — they began to work on "the story." As they lay next to each other on the grass with the evening sun working hard to dry them out, Mark asked, "So, what are we going to tell our parents?"

Lisa replied immediately, "We'll tell them that I fell in the pond and you pushed me back out, and then I threw you some vines so that you could get out too."

"But that's the truth," Mark protested.

Lisa turned her head to look at him for a moment and asked, "Well, what else would we tell them?"

The idea of telling the truth to his parents was a complete novelty to Mark, who had always assumed that anything negative that happened to him had to be hidden with the utmost care. He saw the complete lack of fear in her pretty green eyes and felt invincible himself. So, in response, he shrugged and said, "OK."

They lay there in silence for a short while, and then Lisa said, "Today's my birthday."

Mark, for want of something better to say, replied, "Happy Birthday. I'll catch you a frog if you want."

Lisa shook her head beside his and said, "No thank you. No more frogs today please."

There was more silence and then she said, "I want to spend all my birthdays with you."

Mark, always the lady killer, replied, "OK."

Later in the evening, Mark's mother called out to them from the house and said that it was time for dinner. As they approached the house, Mark began to have second thoughts about this radical new idea of honesty with parents.

They entered the house and stood side-by-side at the edge of the dining room. The adults were all busy setting the table and discussing how expensive gasoline was becoming these days. Eventually, one by one, all four of the adults saw them standing there encrusted with dried mud. Lisa's mother was the first to speak.

"Oh my deary, what happened to you two?"

Lisa answered demurely, "I fell in the water and Mark saved me."

Mark steadied himself for the inevitable retribution he was bound to get for letting something bad happen, but none ever came. Instead, he got... praise?

Now buoyed by this initial success of telling the truth, Mark began to recount the whole story in great detail while acting it out excitedly, including diving off the couch and pretending to lose his shoes in a pile of cushions that he had dumped onto the floor in order to simulate the pond. Lisa giggled during the whole ad-hoc play.

After Mark finally finished his story and replaced all the pillows on the couches, his mother (being a professional photographer) could not pass up an opportunity to practice her craft. Despite her husband's insistence that dinner was getting cold, she took the children out back and posed them in front of the pond. Then, pausing only to slick down Mark's cowlick with a wet finger, proceeded to use an entire roll of film.

After the third picture, Mark turned to Lisa and said, "I knew we were going to be punished." His mother yelled at him and told him to be still, but Lisa had laughed so it had been worth it.

Eventually, the kids were washed, dinner was reheated and ate, and the day was at an end. The adults and the children said their separate goodbyes, and from that day on, Lisa and Mark were inseparable.

A week later, Both Mark and Lisa received a copy of one of the pictures. It was a simple one of them standing beside each other while holding hands in front of the pond.

They each cherished that picture, and each one put it in a special place. Lisa put hers in the corner of her bedroom mirror so that she could look at it every morning when she brushed her hair, while Mark kept his in a little toy safe next to his prized Michael Jackson chocolate bar and a piece of fool's gold that his uncle had given him a year ago.

CHAPTER 48

Mark and Lisa remained close all through both grade school and high school. When it was time to go off to college, Mark followed Lisa to Stanford even though he had also been accepted to MIT and would have preferred to have gone there. However, being a gentleman, Mark never let Lisa know about this, which was just as well because, as it turned out, Mark ended up being very pleased with Stanford's biological curriculum and therefore never regretted his choice.

As for Lisa, she had two great passions in her life apart from Mark: chemistry and biology. Like Mark, she too had compromised when she majored in biology in order to be in more of Mark's classes, although she had secretly preferred chemistry. This was only a small concession, however, since chemistry and biology go hand-in-hand. Lisa had simply chosen chemistry as her minor and never looked back.

After college, Mark and Lisa married and bought a home together. Mark had been fortunate enough to land a cushy (and well paying) job at a research facility run by his old classmate, so they were able to afford quite an impressive house in an area peopled mainly by celebrities.

In reality, they probably could not have afforded the house even with Mark's impressive salary had it not been for the heavy discount the realtor had given them because the place was allegedly haunted. As it happened, they never actually encountered the ghost themselves. They found this somewhat curious until one day Mark did some digging and found out why.

As it turned out, the house had belonged to a friend of the realtor, and according to Mark's new neighbors, they used to have drug parties there and had often come running outside at odd hours of the night while screaming about being chased by ghosts — much to the annoyance of said neighbors.

After learning this, they both felt more at ease about the house and Mark was able to concentrate on his new job without worrying about Lisa while she stayed home to set up their new home.

Lisa would have preferred to unpack and decorate the house together with Mark, but she understood that his new boss was anxious for him to start, and Mark could hardly say no after receiving such a generous signing bonus.

As a thank-you to Lisa for being so understanding, Mark used most of his signing bonus to get Lisa started in her own veterinary clinic.

At first everything seemed perfect between the two of them, but between Mark's new job and Lisa's new business, some stress began to build up between them. It was not distance, but the threat of distance that was the cause. It was the stress of being pulled apart in separate directions.

A lot of this unwanted separation anxiety was due to Mark having to work so much overtime in order to get his project up to speed. Outwardly, it appeared to affect Lisa more than Mark because she tended to complain about it more, whereas Mark truly suffered more because he knew that he was actually the cause. This all might have been OK, but things took a turn for the worse on Lisa's Birthday.

Mark was just walking through the door on his way to work when Lisa called out to his back, "I thought we were going to do something for my birthday."

"Absolutely," answered Mark. "This weekend. I have everything planned out. You're going to love it."

Lisa looked down. "But today is my birthday."

"I know, sweetie. I'm sorry, but today is the big day. We are doing our big demo today. There is no way I can't go to work today. I have to go."

Lisa looked back up, straight into Mark's eyes. "Please. I shouldn't have to beg you to be with me on my birthday. We are always together on my birthday. Always. Ever since we were little."

"I know, but maybe it's time to grow up a little, don't you think? Look, this is it. Today is the day. The last few months of me working my ass off and us not seeing enough of each other were all for this day. After today, we can have a life again."

"Yes, but why does it have to be today? You are the project

manager. Can't you move it to tomorrow or next week?"

"No, I really can't. It took a lot of preparation to set up for today. We have people from the government flying in. It's a pretty big deal. I can't just blow it off or move it. I'm sorry."

Lisa was almost convinced but then she realized something. "You forgot, didn't you? I get that you can't move the date now, but you sure as hell could have chosen a different date for the demonstration than my birthday. You actually forgot that it was my birthday, didn't you? Didn't you?"

This time, Mark looked down. He exhaled audibly. "I'm sorry. I wasn't even thinking. Today just fit so perfect with everyone else's schedules. By the time I realized it, it was too late to change it."

"Everyone's schedule but mine, that is. You actually forgot about me. We used to be practically one person, and now, you forgot about me." In between heavy sobbing she added, "I'm going home. I hope your test subject drops dead. I hope you drop dead too." She pushed past him and got into her car. She sat there for a minute while she dried her tears.

Mark felt queasy. He was so torn. He had to go to work. He had to. If he did not, he would absolutely lose his job. But something in the back of his head was telling him it was important to stop Lisa from leaving. He watched as she started to back down the driveway. His legs twitched as if he were about to run after her, and just then a remnant of a previous life entered his mind. The remnant was an action wrapped in strong emotion, and it commanded Mark to stop that car at all costs.

The twitching in his legs turned into a full sprint. He beat Lisa's car to the end of the driveway and jumped behind it as Lisa continued to back up. Both the car and Mark met at the end of the driveway and said hello. Mark went down just as Lisa practically pushed the brake pedal through the floorboard.

Lisa wrenched at the emergency brake and sprinted out of the car. She found Mark behind the car, laughing and apparently unhurt. She was unsure whether to be relieved or annoyed.

"That's not funny, Mark," she wailed.

Tears of relief trickled down Mark's face. He shook his head in exasperation and said hoarsely, "I'm just happy you're alive."

"Me?" asked Lisa, perplexed. "What do you mean?"

Mark suddenly looked puzzled. "I don't really know. I just had this terrible sense of déjà vu — like something dreadful was going to happen to you if you left. Anyway, forget about that.

Just please stay with me. I'm not going to work. We'll go anywhere you want."

Lisa, who was already kneeling down beside him, bent over Mark and gave him a kiss while her hair tickled his nose. After the kiss, she asked, "But won't you lose your job?"

Mark made a face. "What? You're going to pretend to be the sensible one now? Forget the job. I'll find another one. There are plenty of other jobs but only one Lisa."

Lisa smiled and gave Mark another kiss, this time putting her weight on top of him. Mark grabbed her arms and gently pushed her away.

"What?" she asked in surprise.

Mark grimaced and said, "Sorry, nothing personal, but I think my rib might be broken."

In the end, they spent most of the rest of the day at the hospital, but at least they were together.

CHAPTER 49

───────▼───────

"Oh my god, Mark, look at the paper," said Lisa while suddenly thrusting a paper between Mark's face and the kitchen table.

Mark carefully placed the spoonful of cereal he had been about to eat back into the bowl as best he could and then read the article she was pointing at.

Mark read for about thirty seconds and then said, "Holy crap. Steve Bestiality is dead?"

"Did you notice where he died?" Asked Lisa.

Mark read that part again. "It says he was killed by a drunk driver yesterday morning right down the road from here. Isn't that intersection in the direction of your parents house?"

Lisa nodded slowly.

"That could have been you. It was right at the same time that you were trying to leave," he added.

Lisa continued to nod and then she said, "I'm starting to give your déjà vu yesterday a lot more credence now. That makes twice that you saved my life."

Mark said, "Yes, and twice for you."

Lisa looked puzzled. "When was the second time?"

Mark smirked and said, "When you slammed on the brakes instead of the gas."

Lisa laughed. "I'm not sure that counts."

Mark shrugged. "Well, I think we'll count it but maybe it gets an asterisk beside it, you know, like when a home run is made by someone suspected of steroid use."

Lisa giggled again and said, "OK."

Mark took a deep breath. "Wow, so I wonder what this means for AccelTech? Hey! Maybe I still have a job. After all, no one has officially fired me."

Lisa replied, "I guess you better get dressed and get your

butt to work then, hadn't you?"

"I guess so," replied Mark. "But first, I'm going to finish my Frosted Flakes. After all, I'm already late. Might as well arrive with a clear head and a full stomach."

CHAPTER 50

When Mark finally did make it into work, he was immediately sent home by a couple of the higher-ups. They told him that things had suddenly become very complicated and that they would contact him and the rest of the staff once things were straightened out.

Mark later found out that things had indeed become complicated. A flood of litigation had erupted between AccelTech, the government of the United States of America, and Mrs. Bastille. As a result, all work at AccelTech had been halted until further notice.

According to Steve's will, the company was to go to his wife. The only problem was that Steve had been in the process of changing his will because he had a suspicion that his wife had been having an affair. Unfortunately, in the unfinished version of the will, it was not stated who would get the company, only that it should not go to his wife. Since Steve himself had no children and no siblings, this would mean his parents (actually, his mother since his father was also deceased) would get the company.

Then the government entered into the picture and made things even muddier. The government had contracts with AccelTech, but they did not actually own any controlling interest in the company. However, there was language in the contracts that seemed to suggest that much of the intellectual property developed as a direct result of the funding they had provided would revert to them if the company were to close down.

Steve's wife had no intention of running the company and wanted to sell it, only she did not want to sell it to the government because they were offering a paltry amount since they already assumed they had a legal right to the company's intellectual property. Unfortunately for her, the company was virtually worthless without the intellectual property, which meant that she could do nothing with it until the dispute could be settled.

The government was not entirely happy with their chances of winning the dispute so they also pursued ownership via another route. They approached Steve's mother and convinced her to contest the old will and insist that the latest will was the valid one despite appearing to be incomplete. If nothing else, it was evidence that Steve had wished for his wife not to own the company and could therefore be looked at as a supplement to the original will with this exclusion in mind.

While they had only offered her the same six-figure amount that they had offered Steve's wife, this sum meant much more to a woman living on a fixed income. When coupled with the offer to handle all the legal work and expenses that accrued from the lawsuit, it was an offer she could not refuse.

And so, the fight over AccelTech soon spiraled out of control and lasted a number of years. Matters were complicated even further when it appeared that Steve's wife, Mrs. Bastille, had committed suicide — although according to her friends she was not a gun owner and had not been acting out of the ordinary in the days leading up to her death.

Shortly after her death, AccelTech was burned to the ground in a fire — which was a difficult thing to happen by accident to a building made of concrete and steel. It had been a clear case of arson, but there was insufficient evidence to convict the prime suspect, a test pilot for the former company who had been seen with Mrs. Bastille on several occasions after Steve's death.

The government did what it could to reassemble the former "Plan A" team members, but of the ones that took the offer, none of them had the drive and creative spark needed to fill Steve's shoes and they were never quite able to create even a partially functional Flicker Suit. This actually came as a relief to many of the white coats involved because when it came right down to it, even if they had managed to get a suit working, none of them wanted to be the test pilot.

CHAPTER 51

---▼---

The doorbell rang. Mark called up to Lisa, "I'll get it." He tossed the TV remote onto the cushion next to him and went to answer the door.

"Oh, dude, it's you!" exclaimed Mark after opening the door. "Come on in. How have you been?"

"Ah, you know me — living the dream," replied Pryb while walking through the doorway.

They went to the den and settled into two comfy leather chairs. Mark asked, "Hey, did you hear the news? AccelTech burnt to the ground. Can you believe it?"

Pryb nodded his head and said, "Yeah, sorry about that."

Mark shrugged. "Eh, no big deal. I'm happy where I'm at now."

"That's good."

"Oh," said Mark suddenly. "Did Brad ever get a hold of you? I hope you didn't mind me giving him your info. He seemed really bummed about the death of Steve's ex-wife. Can you believe those two had a thing? Anyway, I thought you might actually be better at cheering him up than me, and I know you used to say that you wanted to have a beer with him whenever I told you about him."

Pryb waved his hand and said, "Nah, that's cool. It was a good call. We hit it off, and I was able to help him with some stuff."

"Oh good," replied Mark. And then he thought about the wording and asked, "What stuff?"

"Oh, just some... redecorating."

Mark stared at him.

Pryb stared back. Eventually Pryb said, "Look, I did just say that I was sorry. Now, let's say no more about it."

Mark laughed and shook his head. "It's a small world," he said, "and life certainly is full of surprises."

"For sure," Pryb agreed. "Say, speaking of small worlds, you remember your friend Samantha from AccelTech?"

"I wouldn't really call her a friend," Mark replied. "She was just my lead assistant."

Pryb continued, "Well, Brad ran into her at the bowling alley and guess who she was with?"

"Bill Clinton?" Mark hazarded.

Pryb laughed. "No, not even close. Not by a long shot. Apparently she hooked up with that frumpy secretary you used to tell me about — the one with the lone cat picture on her desk. Doris? Darlene?"

"Doreen," confirmed Mark. "Really?" His face went through several iterations of puzzlement as he tried to picture this. Finally, he said, "Get out of town."

"It's a mad, mad world," said Pryb while shaking his head.

"It certainly is," agreed Mark.

"Speaking of which," Pryb added, "Brad is now dating that Tammy girl that was always hitting on you. I saw her at his house. Not a bad number. A little hairy, but I wouldn't say no to her."

"I'm sure you wouldn't," Mark joked.

"Yeah, well, a carpet installer always stretches what he lays," replied Pryb.

Mark had heard the joke a number of times before and simply shook his head.

Just then, Lisa popped into the den with three beers. She opened them and passed one to each of the men, keeping the last for herself.

Pryb watched her drink and said, "I don't know how you keep your figure, girl."

Lisa finished drinking and said, "Well, despite its dark color which hints of robustness, Guinness beer is surprisingly low in calories. That, and I sweat like a whore in church while working out downstairs in the gym."

Mark frowned and said to Pryb, "I wish you wouldn't corrupt her like that."

Pryb said with injured innocence, "Me? That is totally your doing."

They all laughed. Lisa noticed the newspaper on the table and read the headline. She said, "Wow, that place actually burned down, huh? That must have been difficult." She turned to Pryb and asked, "Was that your work?"

Pryb looked startled. He composed himself and replied, "Jesus, woman, you should know better than to ask direct questions of a man like me. It's bad for my health."

Lisa continued undeterred, "It's just that it says here that the arsonist most likely used hundreds of pounds of thermite which reduced the building to something approaching molten lava, and I thought that sounded like your style."

Pryb squinted at her and said, "I certainly have no idea what you are talking about, but if I were to perpetrate such a crime, I'd imagine that my thoughts on the matter would be along the lines of 'Go big or go home.'"

"Apparently the whole complex melted down into its own basement," Lisa added.

Mark asked in surprise, "That place had a basement?"

"Not anymore," replied Pryb with a smirk.

The three of them laughed at this and then Pryb adeptly changed the subject by asking, "So, what's new at the vets?"

Lisa, who was always happy to talk about her work, replied, "It's doing really well. We are in the middle of expanding again. Ever since Mark started working with us, the place has been busy, busy, busy. With my surgery skills and knowledge of medicines, and his mastery of nutrition, our patients' recovery rate has earned us a great reputation. In fact, Mark is even launching his own brand of pet food."

Mark nodded at this and added, "I wanted to call it 'Puppy Uppers,' but Lisa said it sounded like a narcotic so the dog food is going to be called 'Peppy Puppy' and the cat food will be 'Frisky Feline.'"

Pryb said, "You may want to rethink that last one. I can see a trademark infringement in your future if you use it."

Mark looked annoyed. "Yeah, I was thinking the same thing but the name just fit so well. Oh well, I'll think of something else. I suppose 'Kitty Krack' is no good?"

Lisa shook her head.

"Bummer," replied Mark with a shake of his head.

Pryb said, "Well, sounds like you two have things all sorted out, then. But tell me — and I don't mean to pry — but don't you two get a little tired of each other? I mean I know you've always been close, but living and working together, that's got to cause some problems. I mean, I know if I hang out with Mark more than a few days in a row, I get this urge to, you know, sort of give him a shove down the stairs."

Mark turned to Lisa and said, "Remind me to always walk behind Pryb when we're upstairs."

Lisa smiled and answered Pryb by saying, "I could spend every second of every day for the rest of my life with Mark and I would not get tired of him."

Pryb made a fake gagging noise and replied, "Oh my God, Jesus, and little baby Jesus — you two are just too sappy for words."

Mark glanced at Lisa for a moment and then said, "It's not really like that, though. We've been together for nearly two decades now. That might not be a long time to some people but it represents two-thirds of our life. For us, being together is just a natural state of being."

Lisa nodded slightly and said, "Exactly." She then smirked and added, "I've long ago learned to suppress my urge to push him down the stairs. Now it's just habit not to."

Pryb watched as the two began to tease each other. Lisa winked at Mark, who made a face back at her. It was cute... in a too sappy for words sort of way.

CHAPTER 52

———————▼———————

On the anniversary of the 20th year they had met, Lisa and Mark agreed that there was only one possible place they could spend the day together. They ate breakfast together and changed into suitable clothes for the occasion. Lisa was wearing a cute red dress and her hair had been put into long, loose curls.

Mark saw her and said, "You look adorable."

Lisa smiled and said, "Thanks. You're looking very studly yourself in those cutoff jeans and a Super Man T-shirt."

Mark looked down at himself and said, "Well, some things never go out of fashion."

They took the drive to their old neighborhood. Along the way, Lisa had to slam on the brakes when a pack of some ten dogs ran across the road in front of them. The dogs each had a leash that led to the hand of one small girl wearing roller skates. She looked panicked.

Mark stared out of the window at her as Lisa began to drive away again.

Lisa said, "What? Are you shopping around for a newer girl?"

Mark replied, "Yes, funny. No, It's just that I think I knew her from the lab."

Lisa asked, "Do you want to go say hello? I can pull over."

Mark watched as the girl was pulled into a telephone pole and her forward progress suddenly ended. Mark cringed and said, "No, that's alright. She's just someone I saw around."

"Suit yourself," replied Lisa while pressing back down on the accelerator.

About twenty minutes later they pulled into Mark's old driveway. As they stepped out of the car, both of their parents came out of the house to greet them.

Lisa's father said, "Hello cupcake," and gave her a hug.

Her mother said, "Oh my dear, sweet, little Lisa. Don't you look precious? We're all so happy to see you two again. Ah, I'm getting teary-eyed just thinking about it."

Mark's father smacked him on the butt and asked, "How are you doing, champ?"

His mother fussed with his hair and complained that he should visit more often.

After things settled down, the six of them ate lunch together and then Mark's mother took the two of them out back and made them pose again in front of the pond.

As they held hands, Mark said out of the corner of his mouth, "You know, I still have the picture from twenty years ago."

Lisa smiled brightly while Mark's mother took a few pictures of them. Once they were allowed to move again, Lisa pulled something out of her purse and handed it silently to Mark. He smiled.

Lisa said, "Mine got a little worn out, but I was able to scan it and digitally restore it. I laminated it after that for safe keeping."

Mark took his out of his wallet and handled it with the care of a priceless baseball card. In fact, it had been placed in a plastic sleeve meant for one. He handed the photo to Lisa and said, "Mine's original."

They both teared up while looking at the photos. After a short while they carefully handed them back to each other and put them away. Mark called out to his mother as she fussed with her camera, "Mom, I think we're going to spend some time at the pond."

His mother looked up from her work and said, "OK. Don't fall in this time."

Mark and Lisa waved back and then found a shady spot under a tree by the pond. Mark was about to sit down next to Lisa when he noticed that someone had carved up the tree.

Lisa saw him staring and asked, "What's wrong?"

Mark pointed at the carvings and said, "Someone tagged up our tree. What the hell?"

Lisa got up and took a look. There was a heart carved into the bark of the tree, and inside the heart was carved "SALLY + THOMAS".

Mark said, "I wonder what that's doing here?"

Lisa shrugged. "You moved here when you were eight, right? Maybe one of these two grew up here and they revisited it just like us?"

"Maybe," replied Mark. "You know, it's funny but I'm not as annoyed as I think I should be about this."

"Come again?" replied Lisa.

"I mean..." began Mark. He started over, "You know how I sometimes get déjà vu? Well, when I see this it just seems right to me. Something about it makes me happy."

Lisa speculated, "That might just be empathy."

"Perhaps," Mark admitted. "One thing about it does annoy me, though."

"What's that?"

"No one ever completes the equation," he replied.

He reached into his pocket and selected a little-used key and began to carve at the bark. Lisa watched with interest.

After a few minutes, Mark stood back and said, "There. That's how it's done."

Lisa looked at his work and smiled. There was another heart carved into the bark. Inside the heart was carved "LISA + MARK = 4EVER".

Lisa read it and said, "Forever and ever."

Mark smiled. They put their arms around each other and kissed.

True to Lisa's promise, in every iteration of the Flicker World to follow, Lisa and Mark were together and they were happy, forever and ever.*

---

*Well, almost forever. Hundreds of thousands of iterations later, a clumsy janitor spilled his morning coffee over the World Terminal and the simulations suddenly ended. However, Lisa would have been happy to know that as the very last simulation froze and its final image faded into darkness, the very last frame of the simulation had been of her and Mark kissing beneath their tree.

www.ingramcontent.com/pod-product-compliance
Lightning Source LLC
Chambersburg PA
CBHW061133200626
46817CB00016B/1381